S.P.R.U.N.G.

SOCIETY FOR THE PURSUIT OF THE REPUTEDLY UNDEAD, NAMELY GHOSTS

Dear Reader,

We warned you not to open this book. But you had to go ahead anyway, didn't you? We knew you would.

First, the bad news: Because you ignored our warnings on the cover and opened the journal, you've just released all the ghosts that were held captive inside.

Even so, there is some good news. If this journal has found its way to you, it means you have the ability – what we here at SPRUNG call Ecto-Sense – to identify paranormal apparitions such as ghosts. You'll need training to use your ability, of course, and this book will provide it.

Let me explain. I am the Chairman of a secretive society known as SPRUNG – the Society for the Pursuit of the Reputedly Undead, Namely Ghosts. Note I said *secretive*, not *secret*. That's because we hide in plain sight, as do our operatives – past and present. We fiercely protect our secrets and expect you to do the same.

If you are in possession of this journal, it is because one of our operatives identified you. You must be one of the special ones who know that there is more to life than meets the eye and that things are not always what they seem. Perhaps you sometimes recognize a place you've never seen before. You know that cheese sometimes tastes strangely like sausage – well, maybe that's just me . . . You know that sometimes, the hairs on the back of your neck stand up for extremely good reasons . . . It means you have the ability to separate the noise of normal life from the whisper of the paranormal. In short, it means you have Ecto-Sense. Most of us simply call it the Sense.

KNOWN SPRUNG BUREAUS SINCE 1917

SANTA MONICA - MONTEVIDEO - DAKAR - BRIGHTON & HOVE - BELGRADE - SHANGHAI - TASMANIA

And, perhaps most importantly, it means you can help us save Agamemnon White, our precociously talented Ghostkeeper. He's brilliant, he's odd, he is a lover of tuna fish and polka-dot handkerchiefs. Ag's like a son to me . . . and he's gone missing.

You are holding Agamemnon's personal copy of the SPRUNG Journal and Field Guide. Ag will have kept all his case notes on his most recent paranormal investigations in this book, including observations he recorded and collections of relevant artefacts. My hope is that if you follow in his footsteps you will be able to solve the mystery of his disappearance. You'll have to track and recapture the ghosts you released, the ghosts Ag had assembled in these pages. We will put SPRUNG's finest ghost-tracking technology at your disposal. You'll find all the details you need (and some you won't need – be careful where your curiosity takes you) within this book.

I shall also share all I believe you should know about Agamemnon (and quite possibly a few things you shouldn't know – it's so hard to tell sometimes!). Do not trust what others may tell you – they will try to distract you from the path.

Join us. We believe you already have the Sense to be a Ghostkeeper. Otherwise the journal would not have found its way to you. We believe you can rescue Ag before it's too late. And we know you'll take the Society's secrets to your grave – which may of course come quicker than you've been expecting if you fail us (I jest!).

We will be watching you, and hoping that . . . you're OK. At the end, I mean.

With you in spirit,

Jeremiah Goodrough

Jeremiah Goodrough
   – Chairman

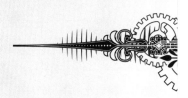 

S.P.R.U.N.G.

Society for the Pursuit of the Reputedly Undead,
Namely Ghosts

THE GHOSTKEEPER'S JOURNAL & FIELD GUIDE

First edition: 1917
Centenary edition: 2017

DEDICATED TO THE MEMORY
OF
MME D'OLIVERA BALDING
1821–1917

JEREMIAH GOODROUGH
1917

INTRODUCTION

Ab Homine, Spiritus

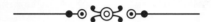

Out of Man, the Ghost. Our motto serves as a reminder that we are all on our way to the hereafter and, just as in life, some are better in death than others.

W elcome to the SPRUNG Journal and Field Guide. This book and the tools we have developed to use with it represent the culmination of a vision created by our guiding light, the remarkable medium Madame D'Olivera Balding. It is with great pride and grave sorrow that I dedicate this book to her — she expired at the very moment her life's work was reaching its culmination. I will always be proud to carry her hunger and passion forward in me.

Madame Balding showed us that paranormal phenomena are not for the superstitious to fear, the occult to celebrate, or for the poet to eulogize. They are not romantic or evil. They are simply here among us, and they need to be engaged and understood. Most are simply troubled spirits, though some are truly dangerous. I speak here, of course, of ghouls. To that end, we at SPRUNG have developed a scientific framework to undertake the capture of paranormal phenomena and use books with unique SPRUNG technology, such as the one you now read, to hold them safe.

With the proper SPRUNG training and equipment, you now have all you need to successfully complete your pursuit of the reputedly undead, namely ghosts. Whether you are a Ghostkeeper seeking harmless ghosts in need of protection or a Ghosthunter tracking dangerous ghosts in need of execution, or even deadly ghouls, this book is your guide and your protection. Use it wisely and it will serve you well. When the book is full of ecto-energy, always return it to the SPRUNG archive for final resolution.

My fellow founders and I will be with you in spirit.

Jeremiah Goodrough

JEREMIAH GOODROUGH
January 1917

3

JEREMIAH GOODROUGH
2017

A CENTURY OF S.P.R.U.N.G.

ELL, WELL. IT'S BEEN A REMARKABLE TIME FOR OUR ORGANIZATION: AND OF COURSE, FOR ME PERSONALLY. SO MUCH HAS CHANGED. YET SOME THINGS HAVE NOT, I'M PLEASED TO REPORT. I AM STILL HERE.

I am preposterously old now, but I suppose one of the advantages of having SPRUNG's technology at one's fingertips is its ability to transform the nature of reality. Lucky me.

Much has changed. For one thing, I'm not quite as pompous as I was when I wrote the first introduction to this book – Latin mottos? How archaic! I've moved on.

Yes, attitudes have changed these last hundred years. And so has the science of SPRUNG. In the first edition of this book, our disciplines and our work at SPRUNG were divided into two approaches: the Ghostkeeper and the Ghosthunter. Simply put, we thought some ghosts could be saved and some could not. However, new psychoanalytic techniques on the living, developed in the early twentieth century by Sigmund Freud and others, began to reduce the number of troubled spirits after death as well as in life. Ghostkeepers were able to use similar therapeutic techniques to understand unresolved issues in a ghost's former life and release them to complete their journey to death. Even the dangerous manifestations of the paranormal that had been the Ghosthunter's preserve were now understood to be treatable. Simply put, ghosts had more to fear from us than we from them. So we disbanded the Ghosthunter discipline and transferred the department to Apparitions Management.

And what of ghouls, you ask? Well, none of our operatives has spotted one in

---

ABOVE: An early SPRUNG prototype device designed by Lily Zhang.

a hundred years, so I think we can just put that rumour to rest. Let me be perfectly clear, ghouls do not exist.

SPRUNG technology has changed, too. We are not going the way of posted letters, newspapers, and tape players! We have created SPRUNG Digital. Using the same techniques we have used for a century to capture the spirit of ghosts, we have absorbed the spirit of the SPRUNG Ghost-o-Matic machinery and other key technology, transferring their essential form and function to apps that can be downloaded to any smart device. Link your download of the Ghost-o-Matic to this book through your personal identification, and you will have the full power of SPRUNG's proven technology at your disposal.

Use that power wisely. Remember you must always return this book upon completion to the SPRUNG Archive for final resolution. It would be more than unfortunate were the journal to be opened by the wrong person at the wrong time in the wrong place.

— JEREMIAH GOODROUGH

IF GHOULS DON'T EXIST, WHY TALK ABOUT THEM AT ALL?

6

ABOVE: *The original SPRUNG Ghost-o-Matic Scanner & Lens.*

SYNCHRONIZE YOUR JOURNAL NOW!

DOWNLOAD THE SPRUNG **GHOST-O-MATIC GHOSTKEEPER'S APP** FROM YOUR LOCAL APP STORE.

FOLLOW THE INSTRUCTIONS ON YOUR **APP'S HOME SCREEN** TO LINK YOUR SMART DEVICE TO YOUR JOURNAL.

ONCE YOU HAVE ACTIVATED THE SPRUNG GHOST-O-MATIC, CONFIRM YOUR LINK BY ENTERING **YOUR UNIQUE IDENTIFIERS** ON THE PROFILE PAGE.

THE SPRUNG LOGO BELOW IS IMBUED WITH ECTO-ENERGY. ONCE YOUR DEVICE IS CALIBRATED, **HOLD IT OVER THE LOGO** TO CONFIRM CORRECT GHOST REVELATION.

GHOST-O-MATIC
HEALTH & SAFETY GUIDELINES

1. The original SPRUNG Ghost-o-Matic device was developed from experiments and observations conducted at the ophthalmology practice of meta-scientist Dr. Lily Zhang in Shanghai.

FUNCTIONS OF THE SPRUNG GHOST-O-MATIC DEVICE

A. *Luminous Ecto Nexus Sensor (LENS)*
B. *Apparition Scanner*
C. *Ecto-Energy Manipulator*
D. *Unresolved Spirit Short-term Storage*
E. *On/Off Switch*

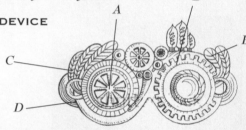

NOTE: THE SPIRIT OF THE PHYSICAL **SPRUNG** GHOST-O-MATIC DEVICE HAS NOW BEEN METICULOUSLY TRANSPORTED INTO THE GHOST-O-MATIC APP. THE APP DELIVERS COMPLETE SYNCHRONIZATION WITH THE GHOSTKEEPER'S JOURNAL WHILE ALSO ALLOWING THE MODERN **SPRUNG** OPERATIVE MORE DISCREET USAGE OPTIONS IN THE FIELD.

2. The smartphone containing the SPRUNG Ghost-o-Matic app is best deployed roughly 30 centimetres from the eye and a minimum of 45 centimetres from the ecto-imbued material such as this Journal.

30cm

45cm

Vertical

3. The Ghost-o-Matic Ecto-Energy Manipulator can be controlled by applying gentle pressure with finger or thumb to the indicated area of the glass screen.

4. A tablet-style device may be used with the SPRUNG Ghost-o-Matic, but only in VERTICAL orientation. This is essential for correct registration of your SPRUNG membership and identity.

ENTER YOUR PERSONAL PROFILE INFORMATION IN THE SPRUNG GHOST-O-MATIC APP NOW. FOLLOW ON-SCREEN INSTRUCTIONS. CONFIRM SUCCESSFUL DATA ENTRY BY SCANNING THE PROFILE PAGE OPPOSITE.

5. SPRUNG Ghost-o-Matic Ecto-Spectacles are currently in development in the SPRUNG Department of Meta-Sciences – practical and elegant ghostkeeping in the years to come.

THIS SPRUNG GHOSTKEEPER'S JOURNAL
IS POSSESSED BY:

NAME

STATUS

DATE OF BIRTH

ALIVE, DEAD, OR UNDEAD

FIRST PET

PLEDGE:

BEING OF RELATIVELY SOUND MIND AND
BODY, I HEREBY PLEDGE TO KEEP THE
SECRETS OF THE SOCIETY SAFE, WHETHER
I AM ALIVE, DEAD, OR UNDEAD.

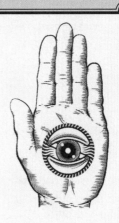

SIGNED: ....

CONTENTS

The sections on ghouls from the 1917 edition are gone!

INTRODUCTION TO GHOSTKEEPING

ongratulations!
You are a SPRUNG
ghostkeeper.

Your service as a Ghostkeeper will be short but intense, like the career of a professional athlete. Ecto-Sense is strongest in the young – this is why SPRUNG is always recruiting new field operatives like you. Make the most of your Sense while it's at its peak but remember – Ecto-Sense alone is not enough. The more ghost energy you collect, the greater your power over the Spirits you encounter and therefore your ability to capture them. This in turn increases your seniority in the ranks of SPRUNG Ghostkeepers.

By the time Ghostkeepers reach 21 years of age, most move on to another part of the SPRUNG organization – for example, Apparitions Management, Astro-Philosophy in the Archives, or Meta-Science and Technology. Many simply become one of an army of former operatives out in the wider world who now serve as talent spotters for potential recruits and lookouts for ecto phenomena in need of SPRUNG's attention. Some are more active than others, but SPRUNG membership is for life . . . and even after it, for some.

You have certainly met one or more of our former operatives – they are in every walk of life but remain sworn to secrecy about their service as Ghostkeepers. Though their Sense is not as strong as it once was, they have retained enough to recognize opportunities for SPRUNG. One of our former operatives will have noted the strength of the Sense in you, and instigated your recruitment. Was it your teacher? A family friend? The salesperson in the bookshop? It could even have been one of your parents. You won't be sure – they'll never admit it, and in the end, you know, it doesn't really matter. You see things others do not. That is what counts.

11

ABOVE: *The original Ecto-Typesetter for transcribing the Ghostkeeper's Log.*

HOW DOES THE SPRUNG JOURNAL WORK?

From its first printing to today's Centenary edition, the SPRUNG Journal has been the primary tool of the Ghostkeeper's trade. The Ghostkeeper stores case notes and observations in the Journal, alongside artefacts that speak to the causes of a spirit's failure to complete its journey to the Beyond. These notes and artefacts, appropriately collected, have intense emotional resonance to the ghost and draw its energy toward them. Once lured by these emotional talismans, SPRUNG's ecto technology allows the Ghostkeeper to resolve the ghost's energy and give it shape. The Journal is designed to hold the ghost captive within its pages, under the curation of the Ghostkeeper whose own spirit is linked to the Journal, as yours now is to the Journal you are holding.

Each SPRUNG Journal has space for the case files of five ghosts. Significant research and development when SPRUNG was created a century ago revealed that the energy of five ghosts was the optimum number required for Resolution. The combined energy held in the Journal allows the Ghostkeeper, using the SPRUNG Ghost-o-Matic, to open a portal through the Journal long enough to send the five captured spirits out to the Beyond, where their ancestors await them.

The Resolution ceremony has been scripted and refined based on the experience of SPRUNG operatives through the years. Operatives have found that a Journal with fewer than five ghosts did not provide enough energy to open the portal. On the other hand, the ecto-energy of more than five will destabilize the portal, resulting in failure. The portal will only remain open for a short time. Resolution is a delicate process, one that is always conducted by the Ghostkeeper at SPRUNG facilities with the oversight of a SPRUNG Archivist.

We cannot repair the lives these ghosts have left behind. We can only understand what unresolved issues have kept their spirits from moving on, and use that knowledge first to lure their energy to us, then to contain it in our Journals. It's our final duty to let them complete their journey and leave the unfinished business of this world to the living.

GHOST BASICS

GHOSTS DON'T HOWL AND LOOK LIKE SEE-THROUGH MARSHMALLOWS.

You can't see or hear them without special tools, like the SPRUNG Ghost-o-Matic, though you can often see the results of their actions — a mark on the wall, a spilled glass of milk, a nasty stain. No doubt you've been blamed for the acts of ghosts more than once in your life. We all have, I'm afraid.

GHOSTS ARE MADE UP OF ENERGY.

There are five different kinds of ghost energy catalogued in the SPRUNG Field Guide. Some energy types are more common than others. But whatever their energy, each ghost's spirit is unique, and has unique issues to resolve. It is the role of the Ghostkeeper to find each spirit's emotional touchstones and use these to lure the ghost into the open. The SPRUNG Ghost-o-Matic allows the Ghostkeeper to bring shape and form to the ghost's energy, capturing it within the pages of the Journal.

SPRUNG GHOSTKEEPERS COLLECT GHOSTS IN JOURNALS DESIGNED TO HOLD FIVE SPIRITS.

Once the journal is full, it contains enough spirit energy for the Ghostkeeper, with the support of SPRUNG Archives, to complete the Resolution ceremony and send these troubled spirits, at last, to their final rest.

ONLY THE GHOSTKEEPER WHO CAPTURED THE GHOSTS CAN HOLD THEM SECURELY IN THE JOURNAL WHEN IT IS OPENED.

If the journal is opened by anyone else, the spirits can escape. Equally, only the Ghostkeeper can complete the captured ghosts' journey through the Resolution ceremony to the Beyond and eternal rest.

ECTO-ENERGY CATEGORIES FOR ALL GHOSTS

Information catalogued by our esteemed astro-philosopher, Nettie Dahl. Remember to refer to this guide before attempting to capture a ghost.

PRISMORPH

ENERGY TYPE: Lightwaves

MANIFESTATION: Common

APPEARANCE & RISKS:
A rainbow appears on your bedroom wall, but it's midnight. Your pens suddenly write in the wrong color. These are signs that you're being haunted by a **Prismorph**: a ghost whose energy is made up of **color and light**. They are beautiful and

KINTERGEIST

ENERGY TYPE: Kinetic

MANIFESTATION: Rare

APPEARANCE & RISKS:
What goes bump in the night? A **Kintergeist**. The Kintergeist's ecto-energy can **create movement** in anything inanimate, from a steel beam to a chocolate cake. They can **make an object appear** – crumbs in your bed, a tree across your path, a flying burrito – or

PHANTASMIST

ENERGY TYPE: Steam

MANIFESTATION: Very Rare

APPEARANCE & RISKS:
One of the rarest ghost energy types, **Phantasmists** will leave you feeling damp, clammy, and cold. These ghosts frequently take the **form of water**, like a dew drop, fog or early-morning mist. Phantasmists only **haunt surviving loved ones**, who tend

GHROSSERT

ENERGY TYPE: Biological

MANIFESTATION: Common

APPEARANCE & RISKS:
Foul. Putrid. Gross. Disgusting. **Ghrosserts** can leave all sorts of nasty things in their wake! Germs. Mucus. Blue cheese. The Ghrossert is a **biological energy** that can cause strange behaviour in organic organisms, which includes humans. This often involves

TOXIGON

ENERGY TYPE: Nuclear

MANIFESTATION: Very Rare

APPEARANCE & RISKS:
Toxigons are exceedingly rare, built of atomic ecto-energy. These ghosts are **extremely unstable** and are in a **constant state of explosion**. Don't let the energy type fool you, though; these ghosts don't pose any kind of radioactive danger on their own. However,

mischievous, but rarely cause physical danger. Look out for **unexplainable stains**, sudden **changes of appearance** and ghostly graffiti.

My last encounter with a Prismorph turned my lucky pair of underpants a bright shade of purple - quite fetching!

POSSIBLE LURES:
Prismorphs are attracted to **art and supplies**, **prisms** and laser pointers, **cartoon characters**.

disappear, like your phone, your money, or your favorite T-shirt. Most encounters with Kintergeists are both inconvenient and painful.

These ghosts love to hide my specs on the top of my head.

POSSIBLE LURES:
Kintergeists are drawn to **industrial machinery**, blueprints, catapults and **exercise equipment**.

to be oblivious to the Phantasmist's presence, even if they have Ecto-Sense. A Phantasmist haunting regularly manifests in the subject displaying cold symptoms – sniffles and sneezing.

It's rumored that a Phantasmist haunted the Chairman as a young man, which led to the creation of SPRUNG.

POSSIBLE LURES:
Phantasmists are attracted to **images of loved ones** or objects that were important to them: a bracelet, a watch, a love letter, a photograph.

bodily functions. Be prepared for **inappropriate noises**, **tinted fumes**, and other **bizarre physical deviations** from anyone haunted by a Ghrossert. Primary risks range from mild nausea to extreme embarrassment.

There are 57 varieties of Ghrossert, by my count, which is why I no longer frequent the local chicken takeout place where I counted them.

POSSIBLE LURES:
Whereas most ghost energy is drawn to specific types of object, Ghrosserts aren't fussy. They are drawn to **anything clean** in order to make it less so. Much less so.

Toxigons are drawn back to **radioactive** environments, which makes them extremely difficult and **dangerous** to capture. There are multiple Toxigon apparitions known to SPRUNG that remain too dangerous to reach with current technology.

POSSIBLE LURES:
Toxigons stay close to their source: **nuclear** power plants, **medical** facilities, satellite installations, **missile bases**.

YIKES!

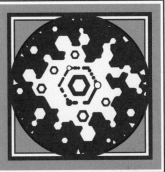

HOW TO CAPTURE GHOSTS WITH SPRUNG TECHNOLOGY

Please study the comprehensive identification table on ghost ecto-energy types provided on pages 14–15 of the SPRUNG Field Guide. Refer to these pages for data compiled over a hundred years by SPRUNG operatives. Meta-scientists have categorized ecto-energy types, recorded spirit-based phenomena, and collected energy samples for the SPRUNG Archives.

However, the basic steps for use of the SPRUNG Ghostkeeper's Journal and GHOST-O-MATIC app to discover, lure, and trap ecto-apparitions in need of urgent assessment and resolution must naturally be learned here and now, or this book could be as dangerous to you as it is to your quarry.

- *Study the patterns of apparition — where, when, and why is the ghost appearing? Unresolved issues from its former life need to be identified and recorded in its Case File.*

- *Find the item or image that will serve as an emotional touchstone and lure the ghost's energy to you. The energy will disperse from the Lure page into the area around you and will be briefly visible.*

- *Use your SPRUNG Ghost-o-Matic scanner to pursue the ghost's ecto-energy. Deploy the SPRUNG Lens to collect the ecto-energy in the reticule of your Ghost-o-Matic device.*

- *Release the ecto-energy onto the Capture page at the end of the Case File. Use SPRUNG tools to manipulate the ecto-energy into its ghost shape.*

- *The SPRUNG Ghost-o-Matic creates 'mechanical' augmentation to complete the ghost's self-image and thus control its energy.*

- *Your ghost is now held within your journal for safe storage until you have captured five ghosts and are ready for Resolution.*

GHOST-TRACKER TRAINING

17

The image on this page simulates a 'Lure' to attract ghost energy.

Set your SPRUNG GHOST-O-MATIC LENS to 'Practice' mode, and let the challenge begin.

GHOST REVEAL

Use this training page to capture and reveal your training ghost.

I promised I'd share what I could about Agamemnon White with you, so I shall write and insert notes like this to guide you as you make your way through Ag's journal.

If I am being honest with myself, I must admit that I am in part to blame for Ag's disappearance. It all started with the sudden passing of Martin McKoken. Martin had been Chief Ghostkeeper at SPRUNG since its inception. Considering all of the unusual paranormal activity he had seen, you would think he would be a prime candidate for an unsettled spirit. But, there was no sign of Martin McKoken's ghost at the event. It was a relief.

Prominent among the mourners were Martin's deputies. Darko Mantich from the Eastern region, and, of course, Agamemnon White from the West. In addition to being our region Directors, they are the best Ghostkeepers SPRUNG has ever had. Ag sat impassively in the front row, while Darko pew-hopped as if it was a dinner party. You often couldn't tell what was going on in Ag's head. His expression changed as rarely as his clothes – he'd dressed for a funeral the same way he'd have dressed for a trip to the mall. Looking at him now, you might have thought his mind was on lunch. But that abstract air was Ag all over. He didn't show his feelings easily. Darko, on the other hand, was an open book – greeting fellow mourners with two hands, like a politician. He was as gregarious as ever, behavior that was in contrast to his somber suit and charcoal cape. Darko looked the part of a Ghostkeeper through and through, whereas Ag just looked like a geeky kid, constantly removing his half-steamed specs and absently cleaning them with a polka-dot handkerchief.

Even though he didn't show it, I knew Ag was shaken by the passing of Martin McKoken. We all were. We hadn't lost a founder since Madame D'Olivera Balding passed at the very beginning of it all. Ag embraced all of SPRUNG as his family and was close to Martin. While many saw Ag as my protegé, it was Martin he worked with day to day – so he couldn't see through his grief, as Darko Mantich could, the opportunity that had opened up for him. So I gave him the push I thought he needed.

Soon, the remaining founders would meet to appoint a new Chief Ghostkeeper to replace Martin – a once-in-a-lifetime opportunity, literally. The obvious candidates would be Darko and Ag, as I said, our best Ghostkeepers, each with the strongest Ecto-Sense we'd seen since the founders were young operatives themselves.

But only one could be Chief – and I confess I wanted it to be Ag. So I pushed him to achieve something risky, even dangerous, but certainly spectacular – to collect the full spectrum of ecto-energy in one Journal, a Spectral Flush. I was certain this achievement would secure Agamemnon White the role of Chief Ghostkeeper.

I am rarely wrong about anything. But unfortunately, I may have been wrong about this.

THE FIVE FOUNDERS

FOUR OF THE FIVE FOUNDERS OF SPRUNG THAT ARE STILL WITH US HAVE LIVED TO AN EXTREMELY ADVANCED AGE, AIDED BY REGULAR EXPOSURE TO THE SPIRIT ENERGY.

Even Madame D'Olivera Balding, who was already old when SPRUNG was formed, lived an usually long time, but still, we lost her too soon. The remaining Founders continue to shepherd SPRUNG as she would have wished into its second century. In these pages they share their combined knowledge of the reputedly undead in all their many guises.

JEREMIAH GOODROUGH

Bravery. Honesty. Loyalty. These are all qualities that our benevolent Chairman Jeremiah Goodrough both embodies and inspires in those around him. The Chairman, already a professor, politician, and eminent scholar of the paranormal, has made it his life's work to find the troubled ghosts of the world and help them move on to the next life. It was he who recognized the unique skills of our other four SPRUNG founders, and in bringing them together, established our glorious institution. Long may he continue his good work. Chairman Goodrough is also rightly commended for his work with the living – finding foster homes for troubled youth.

"Bring me your wayward souls and I shall keep them."
JEREMIAH GOODROUGH

MARTIN McKOKEN

Founder Martin McKoken has served as SPRUNG's Chief Ghostkeeper since its inception. The McKoken family has long been known for its abilities in non-verbal communication – a McKoken ancestor was rumored to have been a world-champion charades player – giving them advanced capabilities in communicating with ghosts. Martin views his ability to help ghosts with their unresolved issues as a form of therapy and psychology. It was this thinking that has led to SPRUNG's current approach to helping the undead and our modern era of Ghostkeepers.

"Ghosts are no different than you or I, all they want is to be heard."

MARTIN McKOKEN

MM - R.I.P. 2017.

HE FACED DOWN ENDLESS GHROSSERTS AND AT LEAST 3 TOXIGONS, YET HE CHOKED ON A BREATH MINT. I SHALL MISS HIM.

20

NETTIE DAHL

If you need to know your Kintergeists from your Prismorphs then you need SPRUNG founder Annette "Nettie" Dahl, SPRUNG's Astro-Philosopher in Residence and Head Spiritual Archivist. Nettie does not have Ecto-Sense herself – remarkably, she is able to channel the Sense of others when in physical contact with them. This allows her to focus the sensations much more precisely than any regular SPRUNG operative. It led to her lifelong obsession with cataloguing instances of strange ethereal phenomena in the SPRUNG Ecto-Energy Categorization System. She and her SPRUNG archivists have catalogued 1,500 different varieties of ghost within the five ecto-energies and are discovering additional ones every day! Nettie also DJs at secret gigs often held in crypts and loves musical theatre.

"There are no ghost varieties I haven't seen – I just haven't named them all yet." NETTIE DAHL

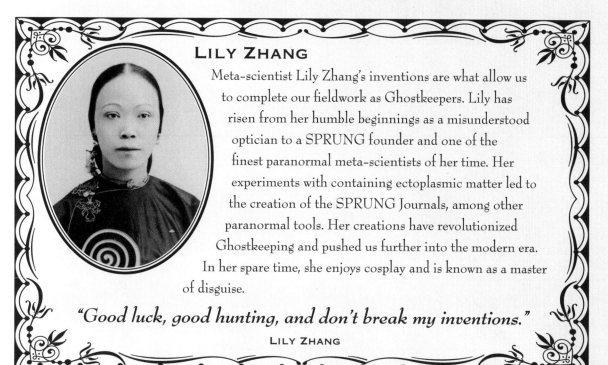

LILY ZHANG

Meta-scientist Lily Zhang's inventions are what allow us to complete our fieldwork as Ghostkeepers. Lily has risen from her humble beginnings as a misunderstood optician to a SPRUNG founder and one of the finest paranormal meta-scientists of her time. Her experiments with containing ectoplasmic matter led to the creation of the SPRUNG Journals, among other paranormal tools. Her creations have revolutionized Ghostkeeping and pushed us further into the modern era. In her spare time, she enjoys cosplay and is known as a master of disguise.

"Good luck, good hunting, and don't break my inventions."

LILY ZHANG

MADAME D'OLIVERA BALDING

Our fellow founder and emeritus scholar, Mme D'Olivera Balding, had a vast appetite for knowledge of the spirits. She brought the talents of the founding group together around her vision of the other world. Her pioneering work in ecto-energy and afterlife communication made SPRUNG's work possible. She saw the possibilities in each of the founders and nurtured them. For example, Mme D'Olivera inspired our chairman to use his fortune for the benefit of the Society and humankind. She recognized the potential of optometrist Lily Zhang to become the leading meta-scientist of the age. The Society hoped that her powerful personality and gifts would push us onward for many years to come. Sadly, this was not to be. MDB died in 1917.

"Life is a banquet of the spirit. Let's eat."

MME D'OLIVERA BALDING

THE ORGANIZATION OF S.P.R.U.N.G.

DEPARTMENT

PROCESS

LEADER

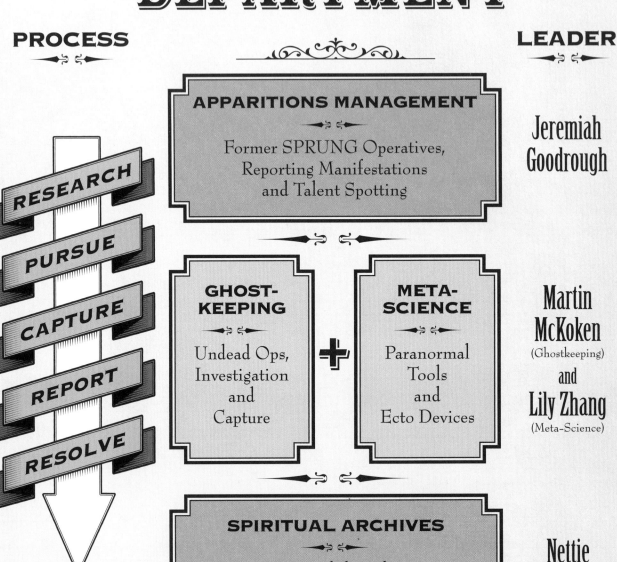

RESEARCH

PURSUE

CAPTURE

REPORT

RESOLVE

APPARITIONS MANAGEMENT

Former SPRUNG Operatives,
Reporting Manifestations
and Talent Spotting

Jeremiah
Goodrough

GHOST-KEEPING

Undead Ops,
Investigation
and
Capture

+

META-SCIENCE

Paranormal
Tools
and
Ecto Devices

Martin
McKoken
(Ghostkeeping)
and
Lily Zhang
(Meta-Science)

SPIRITUAL ARCHIVES

Astro-Philosophy,
Ecto-Energy Categorization
and Spirit Resolution

Nettie
Dahl

GHOSTKEEPING OPERATIONS

REGIONAL SPRUNG BUREAUX & GHOSTKEEPING OPERATIONS

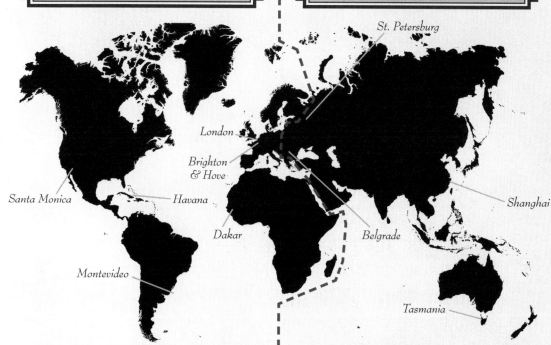

WEST

EAST

St. Petersburg

London

Brighton & Hove

Santa Monica

Havana

Dakar

Belgrade

Shanghai

Montevideo

Tasmania

GHOSTKEEPING WESTERN REGION

Director:
AGAMEMNON WHITE

Known SPRUNG Bureaux in
SANTA MONICA, DAKAR,
MONTEVIDEO, and
BRIGHTON & HOVE

Unknown SPRUNG Bureaux in
LONDON and HAVANA.

GHOSTKEEPING EASTERN REGION

Director:
DARKO MANTICH

Known SPRUNG Bureaux in
SHANGHAI,
BELGRADE, and
TASMANIA

Unknown SPRUNG Bureau in
ST. PETERSBURG.

SPRUNG ECTO-PRINTING

AND THE SPRUNG SYMBOL SYSTEM

SPRUNG uses a complex system of patterns for its symbols, print designs and digital technology. These patterns are capable of absorbing ecto-energy, so that they can be read by the SPRUNG Ghost-o-Matic Scanner and used to capture spirits of various ecto-types.

The SPRUNG logo has various iterations for use in varying scenarios:

Capture of an
ecto-energy
manifestation

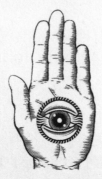

Identification of a
SPRUNG operative

Calibration of
the Ghost-o-Matic
Scanner

SYMBOLS FOR ECTO-ENERGY TYPES

Each ecto-energy type responds to unique patterns.
These are reflected in the design of case files for each ghost type. Examples of these shapes are:

Prismorph

Toxigon

Kintergeist

LOOK OUT FOR SPRUNG MARKINGS ON PAPER, WALLS & MACHINERY

These can be alerts from fellow OPERATIVES, so the SPRUNG Ghost-o-Matic Scanner should be activated and extreme caution maintained.

See sample marking below:

From the moment I met him, I knew Agamemnon White was destined for greatness. Clearly, others did not see what I saw. I find that is often the case—few share my penetrating mind and my unique ability to look beyond the surface and see into what some might call the soul.

Yes, to most people, young Ag must've appeared a hopeless cause, what with his sniffling nose, his spectacles that kept steaming up and the polka-dot handkerchief he used to wipe both nose and specs. Let's not leave out his aversion to eye contact. I remember the winter day of our first encounter perfectly. The details were not pleasant; three of us sat cramped in an overheated office with the fogged windows, plagued by the faint aroma of fish. Me – stylish and charming. The bureaucrat – balding, impatient, and brusque. And the boy – undersized, insecure, and withdrawn. He was ten years old.

The child protection services officer saw nothing more than an unfortunate mess of a child; one who had failed to settle at a succession of homes and institutions; one who was friendless, wordless and seemingly hopeless. He spoke of Agamemnon as if the boy were not even in the room or, at least, unaware of our conversation. True: the boy was perfectly still. Only his eyes moved, following the intricacy of patterns left by the condensation on the windowpanes. Yet, under the desk where he sat, his hands were in constant motion, successfully manipulating the colours of a puzzle cube without giving it so much as a glance. He was distracted from the challenge only by the occasional sneezing fit.

"He doesn't play with the other children," said the officer, reading from a list in the file he held. "He barely speaks. He sulks. That cold follows him around like a personal cloud – we think he needs a warmer climate and a warmer approach." With this, the bureaucrat rubbed his hands together. Whatever he intended to convey, his true meaning was clear: he wished to wash his hands of this lackluster child.

"What happened to his birth parents?" I asked.

"It's all in the file," the bureaucrat replied, handing the dossier to me.

The man was a buffoon. His stories – his complaints – went on and on, but I wasn't listening. Instead, I watched as Ag stared above the bureaucrat's head, where a type-22 hair-consuming Ghrossert was working on enlarging the bureaucrat's bald spot. Could Ag see it? Or simply sense its presence?

Either way, Ag was far from lacklustre. He clearly had strong Ecto-Sense. Add this to his precocious ability to spot detail and pattern, his awareness of the vitality in the inanimate, his obvious boredom with the ordinary world around him, and you had the makings of a superb Ghostkeeper.

All this was evident to me as I stared at the boy by the window. But there was one clue that evaded me – that persistent smell of fish.

"I believe I know the ideal foster parent for the boy," I announced. "A woman who understands children like young Agamemnon here. Jean Beach. She and her husband, Russell, have looked after boys like Agamemnon before. Ones with special gifts who see the world in their own unique way."

The bureaucrat gave me a knowing look, as if my description meant I had grasped Ag's limitations. Of course, it meant the exact opposite, and the boy knew it. Young Agamemnon, suddenly engaged, shifted his eyes from the window to me, fixing me with the extraordinary strength of his stare. He handed me the puzzle cube, I thought to show me what he had achieved with it. But it was in fact to free up his hands so he could pull something from the wide pocket of his coat – a half-eaten tuna sandwich.

Agamemnon took a large bite and chewed thoughtfully.

"Can we go now, please?"

I looked around the room once more. I took in the fogged windows, Ag's steamed specs and sniffles, the sound of running water from the unused sink. There was no doubt about it – the most remarkable thing I learned about Ag that day was that, despite having the strongest Ecto-Sense I'd ever encountered in a child his age, so powerful he could sense without any training the Ghrossert merrily expanding the bureaucrat's bald patch, Ag was completely unaware of the other extremely rare and unusual ghost in the room.

Ag was haunted by a Phantasmist.

ECTO-ENERGY TYPE
GHROSSERT

CASE FILE

The Dentist

CASE FILE: 24761

GHOSTKEEPER: Agamemnon White

LOCATION: Sacramento, California, U.S.A.

PRELIMINARY OUTLINE: 17 November

I am Agamemnon White and I like the number five. There are five digits on a hand. Five founders in SPRUNG. Five cards in a poker hand. I like the way that 5 looks like an 'S' with a severe haircut. So I'm pleased that this is my fifth SPRUNG journal.

I am especially pleased because no Ghostkeeper as young as I am has ever completed more than two journals. Well, except Darko Mantich. He's completed six but he's three years older than me. Not that I'm keeping score.

But scores matter. That's what the Chairman tells me. I might be the best Ghostkeeper SPRUNG has, but it doesn't mean I'll get the big promotion. Martin McKoken was Chief Ghostkeeper of SPRUNG for 99 years, ten months, and three days. I bet he thought he'd make it to a hundred years - it even says he did in the new edition of the SPRUNG field guide, but it was printed months before the actual centenary and weeks before he died. You can't count on anything.

I guess I shouldn't be surprised that some of the founders doubt me. But the Chairman is on my side - he has challenged me to collect a Spectral Flush. This means gathering all five ecto-energy types in one journal. It would be an unprecedented achievement. Darko would be in the shade.

But, it gnaws at my stomach. A massive amount of power will be created by collecting all the energy types in a Spectral Flush. It's dangerous, but it's five ghost types, five Case Files, in my fifth journal. So I was excited to get up this morning, to go to work, to open this journal, to start pursuing the reputedly undead, namely ghosts, and excited I might become Chief. All good. High five!

Except for the fact I'm heading off to the dentist.

INTRODUCTION TO CASE ELEMENTS AND ODDITIES

- *Ecto-activity at the offices of Herve Biensiento DDS.*
- *A part-time dental hygienist and former SPRUNG operative reported paranormal energy on the premises.*
- *Several complaints about 'involuntary and painful facial expressions' to the California Dental Board were ignored. Excessive smiling of patients was not deemed to be a cause for censure.*

Coincidentally, I have been suffering a slight ache in my left rear molar, so this could be doubly useful.

Additional notes:

THIS CASE WAS ON TOP OF THE PILE AWAITING ACTION ON THE DESK OF MARTIN MCKOKEN. JG TOLD ME WHERE TO LOOK.

SUSPECTED INSTIGATING INCIDENT OR TRIGGER FOR EVENTS UNKNOWN

Why are these people smiling? They shouldn't be...

"MY TEETH STILL REALLY HURT"

"I HATE MY JOB"

"I HAVE TERRIBLE GAS"

These people have two things in common: one interesting, one less so. First, I believe they are under the control of a Class 1 Ghrossert, a rather common ghost with biological energy. Notable mostly for the wake of mess they leave behind and their otherworldly control over specific parts of the human anatomy. In other words, they are in thrall to an ecto-apparition, possessed by a spirit, or, if you prefer, they are haunted by a ghost. Ho-hum so far. BUT . . . they all use the same dentist. This is where things get interesting.

PRELIMINARY OUTLINE OF ODD, WEIRD AND OTHERWISE GHOSTLY BEHAVIOR

There's an old joke where a dentist turns to her patient and says, "Open up, please." Then the patient turns to the dentist and says, "Sometimes, I get sad."

See, a therapist will ask a patient to share their feelings, to, you know, "Open up" . . . and a dentist needs a patient to open their mouth to examine their teeth . . . Get it? It's not particularly funny. I always get sad when I go to the dentist.

Of course, people rarely feel happy walking into that office. Dentists appear to have picked up on this, so they provide all kinds of distractions and rewards – the toys in the waiting room, a television to view from the chair, balloons and stickers afterward. But it never works – the only way you leave the dentist with a smile on your face is when they tell you there's nothing that needs work today. Still, dentists want to be liked and try to make amends for the pain they sometimes inflict.

Personally, as a child I found the whole experience complicated. I had often been told to make eye contact with grown-ups, so I tried.

DR. BIENSIENTO GAVE OUT 'GHOST TOOTH' STICKERS. IN HINDSIGHT, AN UNFORTUNATE CHOICE.

Child's dental chart

Eruption (month) — Shedding (year)

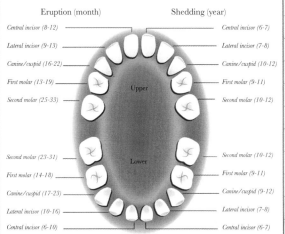

Upper

Central incisor (8-12) — Central incisor (6-7)
Lateral incisor (9-13) — Lateral incisor (7-8)
Canine/cuspid (16-22) — Canine/cuspid (10-12)
First molar (13-19) — First molar (9-11)
Second molar (25-33) — Second molar (10-12)

Lower

Second molar (23-31) — Second molar (10-12)
First molar (14-18) — First molar (9-11)
Canine/cuspid (17-23) — Canine/cuspid (9-12)
Lateral incisor (10-16) — Lateral incisor (7-8)
Central incisor (6-10) — Central incisor (6-7)

Adult dental chart

Eruption (year)

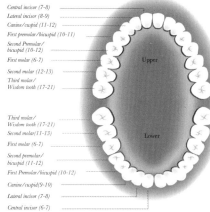

Upper

Central incisor (7-8)
Lateral incisor (8-9)
Canine/cuspid (11-12)
First premolar/bicuspid (10-11)
Second Premolar/bicuspid (10-12)
First molar (6-7)
Second molar (12-13)
Third molar/Wisdom tooth (17-21)

Lower

Third molar/Wisdom tooth (17-21)
Second molar (11-13)
First molar (6-7)
Second premolar/bicuspid (11-12)
First Premolar/bicuspid (10-12)
Canine/cuspid (9-10)
Lateral incisor (7-8)
Central incisor (6-7)

Additional notes:

But the dentist would always be looking in my mouth, not at me. It was disconcerting. And she never tired of telling me what I had eaten for lunch or breakfast based on evidence she found between my molars. I'd always flossed, but she so enjoyed finding food remnants that I took to planting tiny flecks between my back molars, even though she consistently misidentified tuna fish as beef.

From her I learned that a five-year-old has 20 teeth, whereas a grown man has 32 teeth – eight incisors, four canines, eight premolars, and 12 molars. Unless they've lost a few.

But, like I said, I'm delighted to see the dentist today. I'm not having any tooth pain and I have been a dedicated flosser to avoid any unpleasantness at my twice-annual dental visit. So why this extra visit? Because my job as SPRUNG Ghostkeeper is to hunt ghosts. And this dentist's office is haunted. Which is a shame, because Dr. Biensiento is the nicest dentist you could possibly meet.

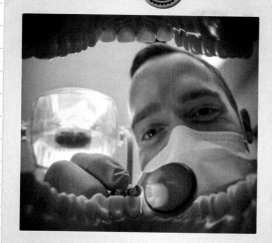

DR. BIENSIENTO– THE HAUNTED DENTIST

Additional notes:

18 November
Sacramento, California, U.S.A.
9:45 a.m.

At first glance, Doctor Biensiento's office doesn't look haunted. The equipment is immaculate, the receptionist is more sugary than a wad of candyfloss, and, yes, there are all manner of toys, magazines, balloons, and televisions available.

And the patients all leave smiling. Which is obviously strange. You may go to the dentist to achieve the perfect smile, but you don't expect to walk straight out the dentist's door grinning from ear to ear.

There is the problem. Dr. Biensiento's patients say they can't stop smiling - no matter how hard they try. Plus, you can see in their post-visit photographs that, even though their mouths turn up at the corners, their eyes show terror. As if they've seen a ghost.

The patients' unusual behavior began three months ago to the day: 18 August. One of Dr. Biensiento's patients went straight from a root canal to her great-aunt Mildred's funeral and was unable to stop her mouth from wrenching upward into a grin. (Though, she argued, her aunt was a miserable woman in her time, so perhaps it was not so strange.) Soon, all of Biensiento's patients began to report aching cheeks and dry mouths, just the symptoms you'd expect from forcing your mouth into a day-long grin.

DEPLOY THE GHOST-O-MATIC SCANNER TO SEE HOW THIS PATIENT REALLY FEELS.

To sort through the nature of this ghostly disturbance, I study Dr. Biensiento's most recent cases. One involved a patient he had seen earlier that month for a wisdom tooth extraction.

In the post-op photo, the patient is smiling broadly, showing a set of perfect pearly-white teeth - but viewed through the SPRUNG Ghost-o-Matic Lens, she looks miserable, as you might expect after serious dental surgery.

My predecessor, the former Chief Ghostkeeper, Martin McKoken, had not gotten far in this case before his sudden demise. But he had left some notes, including a scribble in the margins which seemed to make no sense at all:

"Why the bad breath?"

Additional notes:

PRELIMINARY FINDINGS, SPOOKY OR OTHERWISE

Other than that, Biensiento's patients looked completely normal.

Dr. Biensiento acquired the premises from Dr. Henry Lavage, a dentist who owned the building until recently, despite retiring some forty years ago. A framed picture of Dr. Lavage still hangs in the hall. His own grin is impressive, as is his successor's. Biensiento is a generous man and his reputation for caring dentistry is well known. Within minutes of my arrival - even though he met with Martin McKoken and has asked for SPRUNG's help, so he knows I'm not a regular patient - he has me in his examination chair, insisting my teeth could use a cleaning. He finds tuna (correctly identified) in between my rear molars—and, as I feared, enough decay to require a small filling.

"Nervous? Don't be. It won't hurt a bit."

As he works, the dentist tells me about how everything began to change for his patients in August. Up till then, he had a thriving practice and happy patients, or at least as happy as they should be. But then the grinning started. And there was more - he found his own behavior changing. Biensiento found himself cleaning all the time: at the office, at home, even cleaning other people's clothes.

Additional notes:

"I've been behaving like a chimpanzee, grooming everyone around me," Biensiento mutters as he scrapes at the stubborn plaque on my incisors. And now he's undertaken a renovation of the whole suite of rooms. Once he completes my filling, he takes me on a tour of the place.

The facilities glow with a sheen of clean that would be the envy of germophobes the world over. But the work isn't finished. A hallway leads to a back room, crammed with a wide variety of 1950s instruments, X-ray machines, patient charts, and old patient files. In stark contrast to the rest of the office, the room is dusty, dark, and . . . creepy.

"We've cleaned in here a dozen times and yet it always returns to this state overnight. I can't understand it." Even as he says this, Biensiento starts to wipe at the grime, pulling on a pair of rubber gloves. He offers me a spare pair but I decline the invitation.

My rear molar is growing uncomfortable as the numbing injection wears off. I make my own way to reception, and as I stop at the front desk, the skin of my face begins to tingle. The image of Dr. Lavage smiles down upon me. Soon, in spite of my concentration and personal aversion to the act, I feel a smile coming on. Suddenly I am grinning - grinning so wide it hurts, like my mouth has just finished some grand performance and is now accepting the cheering of the crowds.

 GHOSTKEEPER'S LOG - GHOSTKEEPER'S LOG - GHOSTKEEPER'S LOG

C

DR. LAVAGE:
TOO PERFECT
A SMILE?

23 November
Foggy Bottom, California
   A few days later, I spent Thanksgiving with my foster mother Jean up in Foggy Bottom. Neither of us is American by birth, but we are both very fond of turkeys, so we mark the day together. Turkeys have excellent hearing despite having no ears, like to sleep in oak trees in the wild, and are related to pheasants. Plus, they taste wonderful with cranberry sauce.
   Jean told me how happy it made her to see me smiling so much. I am happy she felt happy, because she does not look well. I know she doesn't like to be asked how she's feeling - as it always makes her feel worse - so I didn't. She seems to have lost some weight and her skin looks pale. I was glad for the moment that I couldn't stop smiling, though my cheeks were starting to burn terribly, as it hid the concern in my face. Perhaps she was just mourning the turkeys.

November 27
   First thing Monday, I visited the home of the retired Dr. Lavage. His residence sits on the top of a hill in a gated community, which appears to have strict rules on the appearance of homes in the neighbourhood. As I walked to the front door, I noted a single blade of grass half a centimetre taller than the rest of the lawn.

HOW MISS MARTHA
MOWS DR. LAVAGE'S
LAWN.

 GHOSTKEEPER'S LOG - GHOSTKEEPER'S LOG - GHOSTKEEPER'S LOG

<u>9:36 a.m.</u>

I'm greeted by the doctor's housekeeper, who introduces herself as Miss Martha and speaks through the centimetre of opened door. A gloved hand appears and passes me a plastic bag. She tells me to place my shoes inside it before entering. I do as I am told, and when she opens the door she receives the bag with a pair of tongs and pops my loafers in a box by the door labeled "CONTAMINATED ARTICLES".

Miss Martha turns to me and smiles nervously.
"What can I do for you today, Mr. White? I'm quite busy here. As you can see, the place is a mess."

From what I can see, the house is immaculate.
I ask to see Dr. Lavage.

"He no longer resides at this address."

"And where can I find him?"

"He can't be found," she replies, and pushes me toward the front door. "You can pick up your shoes from the chute outside."

"Please, I must find him. It's about his surgery. I know he's retired, but . . ."

Miss Martha shakes her head. "Retired? He's certainly retired. He's also dead." I try desperately not to smile at this news, but it's no good. I surrender to a broad grin.

Fortunately Miss Martha hasn't noticed; she's staring aghast at the used handkerchief protruding from my front pocket. I quickly use the offending item to cover my guilty grin.

As we talk, I find that Lavage's life-long housekeeper has inherited the residence. That in itself is not strange, but what is, is how she's dealt with the inheritance. Despite owning her own home, and once being a regular participant in the local bridge circuit, Miss Martha decided to move into the dentist's house.

"The ten-minute commute was just taking too much time away from keeping this place in order," she explains. She lives in the guest suite, and works as though Dr. Lavage were still alive. Even now, she is obsessed with keeping the place clean, terrified of any dirt or mess.

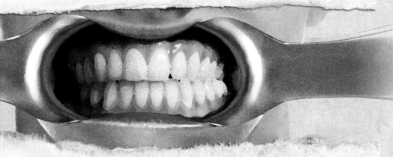

"The doctor had very clear requirements," Miss Martha informs me as she dusts the bottom of a footstool, "and I must say, I am starting to see why."

The house rules are clear and apply to all guests: shoes must be removed and quarantined until properly cleaned or ejected to the street.

A minimum of two coasters for mugs, sanitizing liquid for hands, as per best practice hospital procedure, and an air purifier in every wall socket.

Additional notes:

"He hated taking an early retirement. But his partner said he was so strict in his standards that he was scaring the children. Can you imagine? All because he was too concerned about the damage germs could do. He used to carry a toothbrush with him wherever he went."

"What's odd about that?"

"It wasn't for his teeth. It was for the floors. The man just loved a perfectly polished parquet floor." Miss Martha beams at the memory. I smile back, because I have no choice.

"Without patients, he became obsessed not just with his dental hygiene, but all cleanliness. He saw germs everywhere. It was never good enough—between you and me, I sometimes I think it was a little crazy." Miss Martha tuts as she begins to vacuum the wall.

Miss Martha, after some coaxing, allows me to look around the property, on the condition I wear three pairs of gloves and she can spray my socks with lavender deodorizer.

I walk the halls, scanning with my SPRUNG Ghost-o-Matic Lens. My Ecto-Sense is telling me I'm in the presence of the paranormal, but the Ghost-o-Matic isn't picking up any apparition. I round the corner to Dr. Lavage's personal quarters. If cleanliness is next to goodliness, this place is more than good - it's extraordinary.

For one thing, I doubt that even in the Centres for Disease Control you'd find a room quite as clean as this.

But there's more. The doctor's bedroom is less of a place of rest and more of a gallery. Designed to exhibit teeth . . . His own. A white four-poster bed dominates the room, but the walls, also all white, are adorned with large prints of individual teeth: bicuspids, molars, incisors. Each framed photograph is lit like a Hollywood glamour shot.

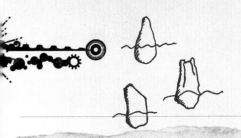

I THOUGHT THE DIFFERENT SHAPES OF TEETH LOOKED LIKE MINI ICEBERGS.

Additional notes:

These teeth are the stars of the show. There are thirty-two teeth in all. The exact amount of teeth inside a human mouth. And to crown it all, there on the pillow is what can only be the doctor's most prized possession. A smiling set of magnificent false teeth.

Also on the bed is a small program from the funeral of Dr. Lavage. The date listed? August 18, three months and nine days ago. The same date Dr. Biensiento's patients began to feel like grinning. Dr. Lavage may have been a dentist, but surely even he did not deserve smiling mourners. What made his spirit even more restless than Lavage had been in life? Is the answer lying on his pillow—that eerie set of false teeth?

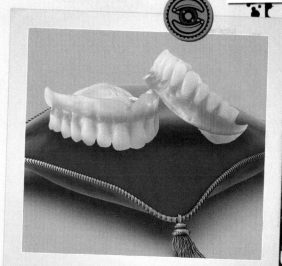

TRUE PERFECTION?

The elements of my first case without a Chief Ghostkeeper are falling into place.

I collect each tooth image from his walls with my SPRUNG Ghost-o-Matic scanner. My own tooth is no longer hurting, but I'm still grinning like an idiot.

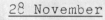

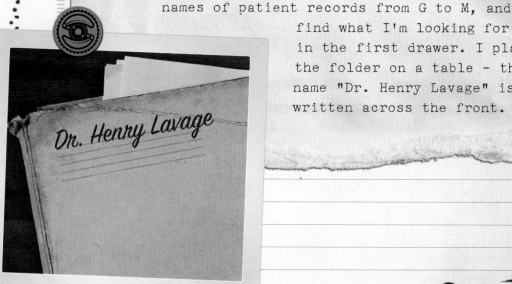

28 November
6 a.m.

I return to Dr. Biensiento's office early the next day. The receptionist is reluctant to let me back into the storage room until Dr. Biensiento arrives. "He was here late, cleaning the freaky room again," she tells me. "It scares me to go in there."

"Don't worry, I can find my own way," I wave off her concerns. "I won't be long."

"Okay, but don't mess it up in there. Doctor B would be so upset!"

I'm afraid Dr. B already has reason to be upset. Once again, the room is filthy with dirt and slime on the walls and floor. But if I'm right, this will be the last time the Ghrossert disrupts his dental office.

And I am right. The SPRUNG Ghost-o-Matic shows the room is shimmering with biological energy, the signature of the Ghrossert, the ghost of germs past and present. I scan the file cabinets, looking for names of patient records from G to M, and find what I'm looking for in the first drawer. I place the folder on a table - the name "Dr. Henry Lavage" is written across the front.

Dr. Henry Lavage

DR. LAVAGE WAS HIS
OWN PATIENT

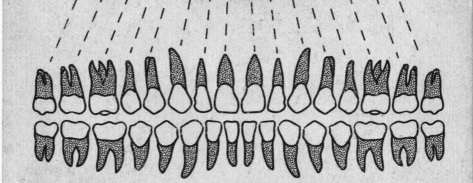

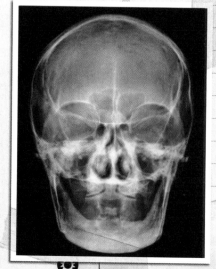

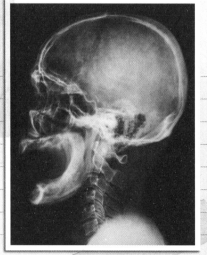

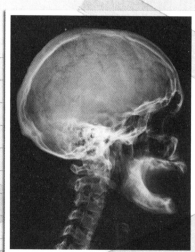

Inside is a complete set of the doctor's dental
X-rays. As I've suspected, his mouth is a black,
shadowy cavern. His teeth have all rotted away.
The Ghrossert haunting the dentist office is the
former dentist himself: Dr. Lavage, ashamed that his
desperate fear of bacteria came too late to save his
own smile.

I am returning Dr. Lavage's teeth at last, all
thirty-two of them, one tooth at a time.

END OF CASE LOG

THE X-RAYS REVEAL THE SAD TRUTH —
DR. LAVAGE'S PERFECT SMILE WAS A
HOLLOW LIE.

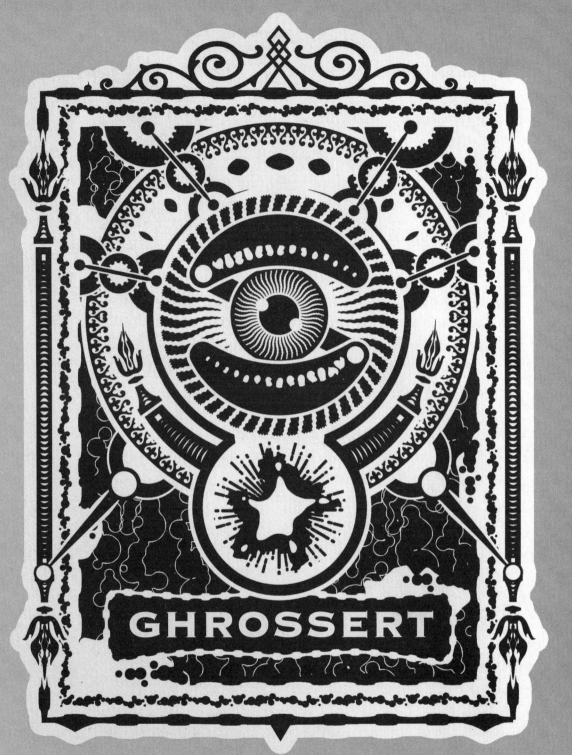

GHROSSERT

GHOSTKEEPER'S FINAL CASE OBSERVATIONS:

- Ghrossert Class A with minor flatulence and extreme repulsion captured. Dr. Biensiento reports an end to spontaneous filth at premises. Unable to convince Miss Martha she can stop constant cleaning.
- One down and four to go.
- Plus . . . I'm not smiling anymore.

'The Dentist' was not a complicated case. But Ag handled it well – as have you,
I see. It was the first step toward the Spectral Flush I hoped would rally support for
his appointment as Chief. Some SPRUNG members felt I put too much faith in
Agamemnon and that he was too inexperienced for the responsibilities of Chief
Ghostkeeper. Possibly. Yet, he had excelled under the tutorship of Martin McKoken.

It was McKoken himself who developed the tools of spirit analysis that allowed
SPRUNG to help so many ghosts achieve their rest these last hundred years. Young
Martin's humane ways ended the role, even RULE, of the Ghosthunter and her
cruel compulsion for destroying ghosts rather than saving them. Martin did the right
thing to push Helani Hekili out of the Society.

More recently, however Martin seemed to become unhinged. You see, Martin's
increasing paranoia about the return of the Ghoul had made him reach out to none
other than Helani Hekili! Martin's recent contact with that dangerous woman and
his 'accidental' death may not have been a coincidence. Never mind. I digress.

I must tell you about Darko Mantich, Ag's rival for the role of Chief Ghostkeeper.
No one respects Darko more than me. He has done excellent work in the Eastern
region. He also cuts a dashing figure in cape and cane, and has endless admirers. I
wonder if Darko needs to remember that collecting followers on social media does
not sit comfortably with membership of a secretive society.

Darko's flamboyance is in complete contrast to Agamemnon's low profile. Where
Darko is self-involved, Agamemnon does not know how to examine himself. If he
did, perhaps we would not be searching for him now. But no – Ag observes the
information around him, absorbs, and processes.

You would be wise to do the same, if you are to have any hope of finding him. You'll
see in the next case that one must focus on small details to find the solution. Look
for the threads Ag uncovered that connect the living and the dead and you will be
able to recover each ghost. With each spirit, you'll take a step closer to whatever
awaited him . . . and you.

ECTO-ENERGY TYPE
PRISMORPH

CASE FILE

The Artist & The Muse

CASE FILE: 24769

GHOSTKEEPER: Agamemnon White

LOCATION: Paris, France

PRELIMINARY OUTLINE: 6 January

The Daily Correspondent Wednesday 4 January 2017

THE DAILY CORRESPONDENT   4 January

Who Was Mona Lisa?

Archaeologist's breakthrough may solve mystery behind Da Vinci masterpiece.

The remains are believed to belong to Lisa Gherardini, a silk merchant's wife, whose portrait was painted by Leonardo da Vinci.

By Isobel Caldwell

Italian researchers edged closer to solving one of the greatest mysteries in art history on Thursday – the identity of the Renaissance woman who posed for Leonardo's *Mona Lisa*, the Louvre's greatest treasure and one of the world's most famous paintings.

After spending four years excavating human remains beneath a centuries-old convent in Florence, researchers have zeroed in on a small collection of bones they believe may have belonged to Lisa Gherardini, the Florentine silk merchant's wife whom many scholars believe was the model for Leonardo's masterpiece. Unfortunately, they cannot be 100% certain that these are the remains of the woman with the enigmatic smile, because the skeleton is missing its head.

INTRODUCTION TO CASE ELEMENTS AND ODDITIES

- The *Mona Lisa* and other paintings have been vandalized with paint at the famous Louvre Museum in Paris.
- The Chairman suspects paranormal activity, as the museum has one of the world's best security systems to prevent unauthorized human access.

Despite Darko Mantich being based in Belgrade, 898 miles from Paris, the Chairman has insisted I take the 5,642-mile trip to investigate this myself.

To prepare, I have looked up the French word for tun - it's <u>thon</u>. I will check pronunciation on arrival.

Additional notes:

INITIAL OUTLINE OF ODD, WEIRD, AND OTHERWISE GHOSTLY BEHAVIOR

Holidays are normally a busy time of year for Ghostkeepers. Ghosts get emotional around annual celebrations and do things they later regret, like hiding the stock of the year's hottest toy or making 'Here Comes Santa Claus' play on a never-ending loop at the mall. But not this year. It's been remarkably dull.

So when the Chairman called me, hemming and hawing until he reluctantly ordered me to fly all the way to Paris for a case that was practically on Darko's doorstep . . . I was really quite pleased. And when it turned out the case involved the Mona Lisa, the world's most famous muse? It was a Ghostkeeper's dream!

FLEW ACROSS GREENLAND TWICE!

MY MISSION: UNCOVER A GHOST OF COLOR IN THE CITY OF LIGHT!

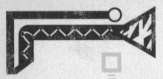

Additional notes:

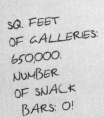

You see, the artist's muse is a sort of a mythical figure. He or she could inspire the artist to create art at the very height of human expression, known the world over, like the painting of the Mona Lisa. But muses are often as unknown to us as the artists they inspired are famous.

The identities of most muses are lost to history: *Girl with a Pearl Earring* by Vermeer. *La Fille au Fan* by Klimt. And, of course, the *Mona Lisa*. A Ghostkeeper knows that being unknown, unseen in life, can make someone rest uneasy after life. While their likenesses are celebrated in paint and canvas, the muses' spirits are unsettled, unrecognized, unable to pass to the other side without the resolution they need . . .

Which is what appeared to have taken place at the Louvre. It seems that Mona Lisa's hair, its canvas under glass and well protected with as many alarms and laser beams as any bank vault, had turned bright purple overnight.

The museum was certain that vandalism was the cause. They redoubled patrols and protections. I was certain that the unearthing of the Mona Lisa model's grave had triggered a fierce reaction from her spirit. When the Mona Lisa's hair vanished all together two days later, I felt sure I was right.

As I said, it was Jeremiah Goodrough, the Chairman of SPRUNG himself, who personally insisted I take this case—he claimed he was doing a favor to a dear friend of his on the board of

SQ. FEET
OF GALLERIES:
650,000.
NUMBER
OF SNACK
BARS: 0!

I WAS RIGHT,
BUT AS I
CAME TO
LEARN,
I WAS ALSO
WRONG...

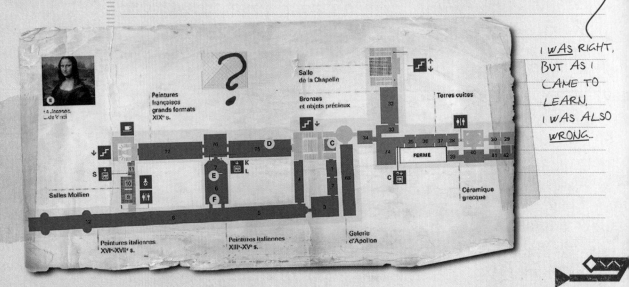

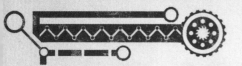

Additional notes:

directors at the Louvre, a Madame Vivienne Dubois, and felt
I would be best suited to the task. I suspected that in truth, this
was another attempt to help me get the edge
on Darko Mantich. Otherwise, why not send
Darko, already in Europe and an expert in
Prismorphs and their haunting colours? But the
Chairman was insistent, so I was on my way
to Paris. And into the past. Even though
I was suffering from my typical Christmas
cold, I wasn't complaining.

MONA LISA (BALD!) ON
WEDNESDAY NIGHT

PRELIMINARY FINDINGS, SPOOKY OR OTHERWISE

GHOSTKEEPER'S LOG - GHOSTKEEPER'S LOG - GHO

7 January
Paris, France
10:30 a.m.

Vivienne Dubois approaches from down a long hall . . .

Her hair sits high on her head, above a long face. She is
a ballerina toy wound too tight - likely to burst into
random elegant gestures at any moment. A grey guard is in
her wake. He has a disgruntled handlebar mustache - and an
impressive black eye.

Vivienne shakes my hand. "The *Mona Lisa* hit him in the
face," she says with Parisian flourish. "It wasn't
deliberate," she adds.

But I suspect it was. It's the kind of thing ghosts do.

We set off to examine the famous painting. As Mme Dubois
leads us up the stairs and on to the Denon wing of the
museum, I note that all of the paintings hang askew. There
are mists of colour across walls and paintings alike, as if
great gusts of paint had stormed through the galleries.

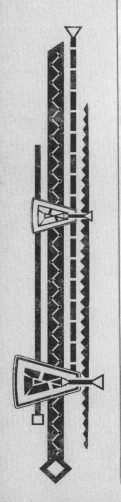

THE 4
PAINTINGS
OF LA
FILLE AU
FAN - THE
GIRL WITH
THE FAN

My palms itch to straighten the chaos. And yet, as we pass the northwestern wall, I spot a series of paintings perfectly aligned and completely untouched by the rainbow tornado around them. I stand transfixed as Mme Dubois and her bruised guard continue without me. I know these pictures well. The master works of Swedish-born artist Gerhard Glimt. They were painted in his Paris studio in the early 1920s. In its original Swedish, the series is titled *Flickan med Fläkten*.

Vivienne has returned to find me: "*La Fille au Fan*, or *The Girl with the Fan*. It is the only work that remains untouched."

The Girl with the Fan is a series of four paintings featuring a woman hiding behind a paper fan. Her stages of movement reveal glimpses of a woman – an eye, a hand, suggestions of shape and colour and mystery. Glimt had many relationships with models in his life – he was a collector of beauty. The girl with the fan, however, was special. I had read that she was his greatest muse. And yet her identity was never known – Glimt passed away before he finished the fifth piece which would reveal the woman's entire face.

Vivienne Dubois sets off for the *Mona Lisa*, but I call her back. "I don't suppose there was a woman who claimed to be Glimt's great muse? This girl with the fan?"

LOUVRE

MUSEE JOURNEE
DATE 07/01/17
VALABLE AU MUSEE DELACROIX CE JOUR
BILLET VALABLE TOUTE LA JOURNEE
9.00 €

LOU:CAS007 14:47
S: 858 T: 479

She raises a brow. "Not one woman," Mme Dubois informs me. She has to shout over a sudden force of wind - seemingly coming from the paintings themselves. "More like 21!" The guard smirks at my surprise . . . till another painting smacks him across the back of the head, and the wind dies down.

Additional notes:

I suspected what my SPRUNG Ghost-o-Matic would later confirm— that we had found the source of the museum's haunting. The discovery of Da Vinci's muse triggered a haunting based on professional jealousy. To the annoyance of the ghost, Da Vinci's Mona Lisa was once again in the limelight. These acts of vandalism were a cry for immortal recognition. Not from Da Vinci's muse, but from Glimt's. From The Girl with the Fan.

GHOSTKEEPER'S LOG - GHOSTKEEPER'S LOG - GHOSTKEEPER'S LO

9 January
7.03 a.m.

Paris is a perplexing city. I have attempted to buy my usual tuna sandwich from a corner café. They look at me with a mixture of pity and confusion. This café is rather quiet. I should not come here again. I eat my croissant with a sombre sort of pride and try not to sneeze too much.

5 CROISSANTS: GOOD
0 TUNAFISH: BAD

I called Lily Zhang from the café. I'd like to say that Lily had always been there for me at SPRUNG like Chairman Goodrough, but the truth was I could never find her to talk in person. No one could - she took this 'Master of Disguise' reputation seriously. Still, she always took my calls. I wanted to know if she'd sent me the Ghosts vs Ghouls document from the original edition of the SPRUNG Journal and Field Guide. Her reaction was typical: "Why would I bother doing that? I invented the Journal, didn't I? So why would I read it?"

She had a point. I guess someone else sent me the extra page. I decided to stay focused on the case at hand.

GREENER
THAN GREEN!

8.33 a.m.

I have now studied the four Glimt paintings at length - the model has become just a blur of colour to me in my hours of staring. Each canvas appears to be linen prepared for oil paint, medium thickness with a fine weave. I gather from their high quality that Glimt spent many francs on the materials to create this quartet. Certainly, more than he did on any of his other works, with canvas of a medium quality. The paintings must have meant a great deal to him - but what of the woman? She appears unremarkable. It's what you don't know about her that makes her so alluring.

Vivienne says that one theory of the girl is she used the fan to hide a disfigured face. Scars? A birthmark or a lesion?

Regardless, her eyes are captivating. They are greener than any emerald - haunting. They would, however, pair nicely with a goatee.

2:05 p.m.

At my urging, Mme Dubois has found fading prints preserved from the archives of the twenty-one models who have claimed to be the girl with the fan. They are, of course, in black and white, as all photographs from that time. However, one can immediately be dismissed. Jean Andouille, the famous Bearded Lady of the Cirque Nationale. Still, I was right about the goatee.

LE PONT DE
L'ARCHEVÊCHÉ
AND ITS LOVERS'
LOCKS.

3:18 p.m.

Paris is a city heavy with love. I walk toward the National Archives to look through census records but find my preferred path closed. A man with a yellow hard hat informs me they are cutting approximately 45,000 tons of locks from the bridge—the Pont de l'Archevêché. It has become so weighed down with the locks of lovers that the bridge is quite literally breaking from the weight of heavy hearts. I find another path and wonder if Glimt broke, much like the bridge, beneath the love of his 21 muses.

Additional notes:

PHOTOS FROM
MME DUBOIS:
GLIMT WAS A
BUSY MAN!

A review of the national census for 1925 eliminates 12
more women, none of whom were living in Paris in the
years when the works were painted. Two more were not
living at all in 1925. Of the remaining six, only three
had green eyes.

This leaves Amelie Raymond, Augustine Faubourg, and
Nanette Gorgon.

 GHOSTKEEPER'S LOG - GHOSTKEEPER'S LOG - GHOSTKEEPER'S LOG

Additional notes:

Amelie and Nanette both passed away many years ago - two women of the same cloth. A dancer and a singer, both famously beautiful and great talents on the Paris scene in their time.

Nanette Gorgon does not appear to have many relatives left in Paris today. Much of her family migrated to London, England, as the Second World War turned out the Parisian lights she loved. According to an obituary in her name, Nanette breathed her last some thirty years ago, in a cottage far away in Lyndhurst, England, surrounded by a devoted family she loved. The timing of her death and the lack of hauntings since then makes me think she is not the cause of this most recent disturbance, but I can't be sure.

NANETTE

When you follow the threads of Amelie Raymond's bloodline, you find another Parisian: Toulouse-Lautrec. He is a spirit SPRUNG kept and cleared long ago - a ghost of color and light. It seems the Raymond bloodline is dusted with tragedy. Amelie was constantly photographed with men - I believe they may have flocked to her, sitting around her like pigeons as she dispensed morsels of bread. She appears to have broken more hearts than there are locks on the Archevêché bridge. And yet Amelie was a hero of the French Resistance during World War Two, finally caught and killed by the Nazis in the 1940s.

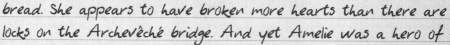

AMELIE

AUGUSTINE

Our final potential green-eyed ghost is Augustine Faubourg, who lived to a very ripe old age, like a great French cheese. Blue-veined and rancid, she bitterly claimed that she was the beauty behind the Fan, right to her dying day, which, in one of those odd coincidences I encounter often in this line of work, was

the very day in September when the Mona Lisa's remains were uncovered, making her a strong contender.

However, to be absolutely certain, I must find those who remember these three women if I am to resolve the disturbance within their spirits. To use the wrong Lure could cause even more jealousy-based destruction upon the Louvre's artworks.

---

10 January
Paris, France, Europe
12.07 p.m.

I have received a call from a Monsieur Nicolas Perdu, responding to my discreet enquiries for assistance. He proposes a meeting at a restaurant called La Coupole. I ask if they will serve tuna sandwiches - or if perhaps I should bring my own. Nicolas laughs - but I cannot identify exactly what is funny. I clarify their policy with reception at my hotel to avoid a faux-pas and am assured that all will be well.

What colors do the hair, eyes, lips, and scarf need to be on the sketch for each girl? The correct combination will surely lure the energy of the ghost, and then I will settle the puzzle and the spirit of Flickan med Fläkten, La Fille au Fan, or The Girl with the Fan for posterity, and give Glimt's muse the recognition she craves.

I NEED TO MAP OUT WHAT I KNOW ABOUT EACH MUSE . . .

	HAIR	EYES	LIPS	SCARF
Amelie				
Nanette				
Augustine				

3:21 p.m.

Monsieur Nicolas Perdu is a little bird of a man. He looks as though he is constantly trying to take flight and failing, much like the now extinct dodo that could not escape its fate. Seafood appears on silver platters. But there is no tuna after all.

M. Perdu worked in fashion as a young man. He was only a boy when he knew Glimt's three precious muses. "Yes, all three were painted by Glimt," he assures me, though that was long before Perdu knew them. ("How old do you think I am?" He winks at me. "Ninety-two," I quickly reply, but perhaps he was not really asking.) The details he remembers about the models are fragments, like painting half a picture. And they are all about their appearance, not their characters. They tumble from his mouth like clothes pegs holding up his memories.

Amelie loved green scarves. So did Nanette. But Amelie also shared clothes with Augustine, because Augustine's best scarf matched Amelie's hair.

Augustine always liked to contrast the colors of her eyes, lips, hair, and scarf, with no two colors the same.

Nanette was not the only redhead in the group. But she always matched her hair and her eyes to her lipstick and her scarf. I quickly grow impatient with M. Perdu's ramblings, thinking little of their value till much later.

TABLEAU DE ... POUR LE MAQUILLAGE DE JOUR

BRUNE — TEINT MAT — TEINT CLAIR
BLOND CENDRÉ — TEINT MAT — TEINT CLAIR
CHATAIN CLAIR — TEINT MAT — TEINT CLAIR
BLOND PLATINE — TEINT MAT — TEINT CLAIR
CHATAIN FONCÉ — TEINT MAT — TEINT CLAIR
ROUX — TEINT MAT — TEINT CLAIR

I decided to make my rapid apologies and depart. I left M. Perdu lost in reverie. I'd had enough of his riddles. Besides, I had one last critical lead. Mme Dubois had arranged for me to visit the caretaker of Glimt's studio in an attic off the Rue des Martyrs, below Montmartre.

11 January, 8.03 a.m.

Madame Fontaine is as wrinkly as a potato left in the oven too long. I approximate at least eighty-seven separate wrinkles on her cheeks alone.

Additional notes:

NOTE TO SELF: PACK OWN SANDWICHES ON MISSIONS ABROAD

THIS INSPIRED ME! EACH ONE HAS HER OWN UNIQUE COLOR SET ...

I STILL
CAN'T
TELL —
IT COULD
BE ANY
OF THE
THREE
WOMEN.

THE CARD
LEFT
BY AMELIE.
OR COULD
IT BE
AUGUSTINE?

XO A

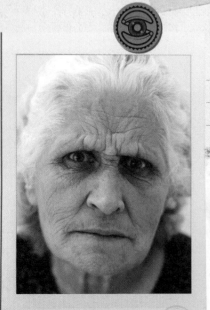

MME FONTAINE WAS
DELIGHTED TO SEE ME...

RUE
DES
MARTYRS

9ᵉ Arrᵗ

The caretaker's shiny green eyes are magnified
by bottle-bottom glasses she removes to look her
best when I take her photograph. It doesn't help.

Green eyes again. Could she be . . . she cackles
at my suggestion and shakes every wrinkle of her
neck, before dissolving into a fit of coughing.
I sneeze in sympathy.

But here is what I have come for - the black-and-
white studies for *The Girl with the Fan*, the only
place I've seen the fan lowered enough to reveal
her face. But it could be any of the three women - Amelie,
Nanette, or Augustine.

Mme. Fontaine remembers all three. Nanette loved to laugh
- as did Glimt. The muse was obviously Nanette! Augustine
was the cool, blonde, northern girl - but Amelie was full
of fire, just like her hair. "So perhaps," she muttered,
"Amelie was the girl with the fan." After all, wasn't
it Amelie who gave Glimt the card with a pink
lipstick kiss and the inscription, "xo, A"?

But as she hands the card to me, her eyes light
up: "But now I think about it, Augustine wore pink
lipstick too. So it must be Augustine!" She smiles
up at me. "Mystery solved."

I nod my agreement, though she has now nominated
each girl in turn. Despite herself, she has given
me the answer though. Glimt had pink, red, green,
and yellow shades on the palette he had prepared
for his final portrait. It still sits beside his
easel, ready for the canvas he never painted. With
the correct combination of colors I can settle the
puzzle and give Glimt's muse the recognition
she craves.

END OF CASE LOG

PRISMORPH

GHOSTKEEPER'S FINAL CASE OBSERVATIONS:

- Two out of five—the Chairman must have known the Louvre ghost would be a Prismorph.
- The 'h' is silent in thon. Useful to know.
- I'm bringing some perfume back for Jean - it is called Number 5, so I'm sure it's nice.

So you have solved the mystery of 'The Artist and the Muse,' as Ag did before you. I have faith in you, as I did in Ag. Don't let me down.

Once I freed him from the child protection services officer, I placed young Agamemnon with a family I knew in the Canyon. Jean Beach had fostered others for me and I knew she would not be fazed by Ag's quirks, or worse, try to rid him of them.

They were a good team, so I was sorry to hear that Jean died recently. I knew she wasn't well, though she didn't want Ag to know – and she was good at keeping secrets.

Jean and her husband, Russell, were in the Society's debt. Years before, SPRUNG operatives had undertaken an awkward case for them. You see, large sums of money kept disappearing from local bank vaults and materializing under the mattresses of Jean and her family. The detective in charge of the police investigation did not believe that this was the work of a malicious spirit and was ready to arrest and prosecute the Beaches, even though they reported every penny they received. I was able to reason with her – not the detective, you understand, but the ghost. A Grade 2 Kintergeist, who in life worked for 43 years as a teller at Anchor Bank and never misplaced a dime. Evidently, in death, she regretted her honesty. While cash continued to vanish from various financial institutions, Jean and Russell stopped receiving unexpected cash deposits in their sleeping chambers and thus were no longer considered suspects. And I was much better dressed from that day forth. But I digress . . .

When I brought Ag to the Beaches, I was unsure how much to tell Jean and Russell about Ag's ghost. Ag himself was not conscious of it – though his subconscious must've been screaming at him. It happens, you know – something is so familiar if it has always been there, so you don't see it at all. And, as luck would have it, the Beach family's own tragic past provided an explanation for the ghost's existence, should such a thing be required.

For the time being, Ag's ghost was hiding in plain sight. And Ag suspected nothing. It would be dangerous for him to know, I felt, for reasons that will become clear as we proceed...

ECTO-ENERGY TYPE
PHANTASMIST

CASE FILE

Runaway

CASE FILE: 24852

GHOSTKEEPER: Agamemnon White

LOCATION: Foggy Bottom, CA

PRELIMINARY OUTLINE: 9 March

MY PHANTASMIST
GALLERY

INTRODUCTION TO CASE ELEMENTS AND ODDITIES

• This case is not officially assigned

Jean was in the hospital when I returned from my trip. I gave her the bottle of Number 5 perfume I bought for her in Paris.
When I returned to the hospital to collect her things, the bottle was open on her nightstand with 53 ml missing, so I believe she tried it before she died.
Of course, it's scientifically possible the perfume evaporated into thin air...

SUSPECTED INSTIGATING INCIDENT OR TRIGGER FOR EVENTS UNKNOWN

This was not a typical case. Not at all. It was too close to home - to be more precise, it was in my home.

When I was a child, I used to draw faces in the condensation on a window or bathroom mirror. When the window steamed over again, my drawing would reappear.

I did this often as I grew - it made me feel less lonely in a foster home full of children.

Sometimes I noticed faces in the window that I didn't draw. As I got older, I started noticing faces in lots of things - a cup of coffee, a steamed glass, a cloud. I was so used to seeing faces in the objects around me that I stopped noticing it, and the act of them existing became just as normal as the clouds themselves. I suppose that's why I never realized how unusual it was to always be surrounded by damp and moisture and faces in the mist.

THIS ISN'T A GHOST...

NOR IS THIS...

BUT THESE MIGHT BE!!

Of course, there's no one 'normal' for all of us. After all, some people don't like tuna - which is unimaginable to me. But I suppose that's more a matter of what we learn to appreciate.

As far as the faces go, there's actually a scientific name for this - it's called pareidolia. It occurs when the mind identifies a familiar pattern in random data. Well, that's one explanation. Now I know there's another. But back then, it just seemed normal. Not para-normal.

And even though it's not normal for a house on top of a cliff to flood, it didn't entirely surprise me when my childhood home did.

 GHOSTKEEPER'S LOG - GHOSTKEEPER'S LOG - GHOSTKEEPER'S LOG

7:05 a.m.

I sometimes sleep with earplugs to keep myself from being woken by my own snoring. So I don't know how long the phone has been ringing, though there were alarm bells sounding in what must have been a dream.

It's Louie Kelly, the Foggy Bottom fire chief. "You better come up the Canyon, Ag. Your old house is under a few feet of water."

I sit in bed, not wondering how the old place is flooded, but how I'll feel about heading up there for the first time since my foster mother's death. I blow my nose - it must be Sunday, as my hankie is the purple one with the pink polka dots. Jean had always liked a Sunday - and felt it should be repeated every other day of the week.

10:15 a.m.

I turn up into the Canyon from the coast, and immediately find the road shrouded in fog. It happens sometimes - when it's hot inland, the coastal moisture gets trapped against the sides of the canyon and it can be as thick as pea soup. Hence the name of the area: Foggy Bottom. My windshield starts to steam up - and, as usual, I think I see a face peeking at me from within the condensation. I'm so busy wiping that I miss the turn-off the first time around.

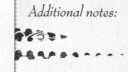

<u>11:19 a.m.</u>
There's so much of this freak floodwater surrounding my childhood home that I can't drive right up to it. Instead, I park at a nearby store. That's where I meet Louie Kelly. We head up the hill together. On top of being the volunteer fire chief, Louie's the local plumber. "If it's smelly, call Kelly" is the motto on the side of his van, and all the locals just call him Smelly Kelly when he isn't around. It's a fair description.

PRELIMINARY OUTLINE OF ODD, WEIRD, AND OTHERWISE GHOSTLY BEHAVIOR

"Here's the strange thing," Louie tells me as we trudge up the dirt track. "It hasn't rained here since the start of March. None of the other houses have a problem; just your old place."

I'm only half listening to Louie, because I'm noticing the ground is getting slippery. There's a trickle of water coming down the slope, though the sky is as dry as a bone.

"I couldn't see nothing wrong with the plumbing neither or I'd have fixed it for you."

LOUIE IS A LITTLE CAMERA SHY ...

The dribble of water is getting stronger, turning the track to mud, and I'm sliding back every few steps. Louie must be used to this kind of thing with all his adventures in sewers and septic tanks. He doesn't seem troubled.

"We were all real sorry when Jean passed, but glad you were the one who got the house. Not all her care kids were like you, ya know. Some real doozies . . ."

I'm about to object when I find myself in mid-air . . . a sudden cascade of water has knocked me off my feet and I'm now sliding down like a Jamaican bobsledder, fast and out of control to the bottom of the hill.

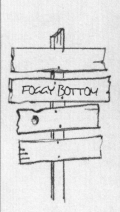

FOGGY BOTTOM

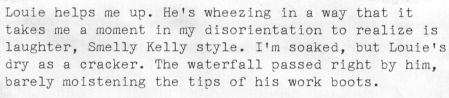

Additional notes:

Louie helps me up. He's wheezing in a way that it takes me a moment in my disorientation to realize is laughter, Smelly Kelly style. I'm soaked, but Louie's dry as a cracker. The waterfall passed right by him, barely moistening the tips of his work boots.

"Something's trying to keep you from the house, I reckon," he cackles.

I sneeze. I sneeze again.

INITIAL FINDINGS, SPOOKY OR OTHERWISE

When we finally reached the house, the door was wide open, but the water was gone.

Everything on the ground floor was damp, even more so than I remembered it being through most of my childhood. Jean was somewhat of a hoarder - but her method had been organized chaos. Now, random stacks of soaked newspapers and video tapes drip from odd corners on to the floor. The whole place smells like a subway.

It wasn't always that way. When the Chairman first took me to the Beaches, I felt like the luckiest kid alive. Every day really did feel like a free, fun Sunday. Of course, back then Jean and Russell were still married and I thought the house was a happy one. Then Russell left and everything changed . . . Or maybe he left because things changed. When you're a kid you never really have all the facts.

I certainly didn't think I had them all now. But, thanks to my training at SPRUNG, I knew one fact for certain: there was a spirit in this house. An extremely rare one, too. Phantasmists are the unicorns of the Ghostkeeper community. Their energy is hard

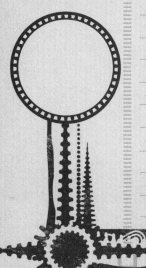

JEAN
BEFORE HER
FOSTERING
DAYS

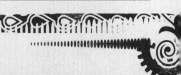

to catch — you cannot see them and can only feel them seeping into your bones. They can form as steam, water, mist, or clouds. Soft rain, rough rivers, or a single teardrop. They are sad ghosts, always. And cold.

I glanced over at Louie, who was keeping an eye out for a plumbing problem he could solve. Even though it was a warm early Spring day, I could see his breath in the air, like you'd expect to see when it was cold. It hit me that even in the hot Canyon summers of my youth, I wore a thick scarf, always finding myself chilly. My current sense of this sad, cold ghost was remarkably familiar. And in some unexpected way, comforting. Had the Phantasmist always been here?

> LAST WILL AND TESTAM
>
> Name   Jean Patricia Beach
>
> 24371 Foggy Bottom Canyon,
>
> Los Angeles and State of California
>
> lawful age, do make, ordain, publish and declare this
>
> Last Will and Testament

It is not unusual for a personal connection to exist between Ghostkeeper and Phantasmist. That's exactly why capturing a Phantasmist can be difficult, even dangerous. Not dangerous the way a Toxigon can be, whose attraction to radiation makes it poisonous for a Ghostkeeper to track, but dangerous because an operative can't form a strong hold over a ghost to which he has a personal link. The Phantasmist doesn't always stay captured in the Journal and that can result in unexpected consequences. I remembered my trainer's instructions from SPRUNG: "Proceed with caution . . . and a well-charged Ghost-o-Matic in your hand."

It was only a few days earlier that I'd found out I'd inherited the old house in Foggy Bottom. I assumed it would go to a charity to fund kids in foster care. Or maybe to Russell, if he was still alive. So when the lawyer explained the will I was more surprised than happy. Apparently, so was someone else. Someone undead.

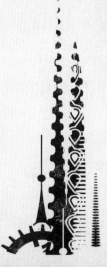

I WAS SURPRISED WHEN JEAN LEFT ME THE HOUSE

10 March
7:35 a.m.

I order an extra shot of espresso in my morning coffee. I'm not sleeping well and my allergies are much worse than usual. My nose is red and my eyes won't stop watering. As the barista hands me my coffee, she grins. "Hey, look at the froth! I didn't even try to do that!"

She's right. There's a milky face grimacing up at me. I'm certain the barista had nothing to do with it.
"Nice," I say stupidly.

"Normally I just do hearts," she says, even more stupidly.

11:19 a.m.
I head back to the old house, this time wearing spiked shoes to drag myself through gushes of thick mud up the hill. As I open the door, all of the feelings I experienced yesterday are back, and much stronger. Someone - or something - has been in the house. The hairs on my neck won't settle. My glasses keep steaming up too.

Beside the door there is a side table with tiny dishes and faded names along it. Out of habit, I put my keys in the dish under which "Agamemnon" can still be vaguely seen. I turn the corner - and find a light on in the closet under the stairs. I tug it open and find a dry box. It couldn't have been here yesterday - the contents would have been soaked. Instead, they are as dry as desert bones. Someone wanted me to find the box when I was alone.

I carry the box down the hill. The journey is easier. The mud less disruptive. It lost its battle.

When I close the door of my car, I reach into the container. At the top I find a chart I created when I was eight, with a strict pattern showing me how to alternate between my hankies, scarves, and undies. I can't help but feel it's too bad I grew out of those ninja undies. There is a picture of me at

THIS KEEPS HAPPENING TO ME

age 14 wearing a goofy hat and a scarf - so it must have been late in the week.

It's all personal odds and ends in the box - the chart, the photos, some old report cards, several coins. Not much to investigate, though. So I head to the office of Social Services.

3:01 p.m.
Social Services for the county is down on Sugar Boulevard and, like most underfunded government agencies serving poor families, has the smell of disinfectant mixed with several generations of hygiene mishaps.

I speak to a Child Services Officer named Leonard Smart, who is not smart in any other way, but he does finally understand that I am researching my foster mother and agrees to provide me with a list of the other children she took in over the years. Jean never spoke to me of my predecessors in the house, though I had seen evidence of them in half-chewed pen tops, scribbles in book pages, and those key dishes.

Yet my own name is not the only one on the list that is familiar, although the other name is extremely unexpected: Darko Mantich. My colleague at SPRUNG.

Additional notes:

NINJA PANTS ... BUT I SNEEZED TOO MUCH TO BE SNEAKY

	Mon						
ading	B B B⁺B⁺B⁺B⁺						

(report card, partially legible)

ading	B B B⁺B⁺B⁺B⁺						
elling	C B⁻B⁺B97A⁻B⁺						
riting	A⁻A⁻A⁻A⁻A⁻A⁻A⁻						
rawing							
rithmetic	C⁺B⁻B⁺C⁻C⁺C⁻C⁻						
rammar	B B B⁻C C⁺B⁻C⁺						
eography	- - B B⁺B⁺B⁻B⁻						
istory							
hysiology	- -						

MY REPORT CARD - I DIDN'T TRY MUCH

Clothing Rota for A. White by A. White

	Mon	Tues	Wed	Thurs	Fri	Sat	Sun
Hankie	Red with white polka dots	White with Red polka dots	Purple with Green polka dots	Dark Blue with Light Blue polka dots	Black with Yellow polka dots	Puce with Aubergine polka dots	Free Choice
Pants	Ninja	Bear	Ninja	Bear	Ninja	Bear	Tidy Whities
Shirt	Blue	Paisley	Stripes	Blue	Paisley	Stripes	T
Scarf	No	No	No	Maybe	Yes	Yes	Yes

AB.C. 0123

PLEASE TURN OVER

TELEGRAM

The time received at this office is shown at the end of the message

T.
C.
B.

Office Date Stamp

| Office of Origin. | No of Words. | Time of Lodgment : | No. |

Cable service to all parts of the world
Time of receipt is set at STANDARD TIME at point of destination

Darko, I need to speak to you about Jean. I'm sure you are aware
of her passing. There are strange things happening at the old
house.
I have a feeling you may know why.-A. WHITE

ANSWER REQUIRED. SENDER AWAITING REPLY.

ALWAYS
COLD BUT
ALWAYS
PREPARED
WITH AN
EXTRA PAIR
OF SPECS
FOR MY
HAT,
– ME,
AGE 14

<u>12 April</u>

The Chairman was late for lunch as usual. I am grateful to
him for many things, but this habit of tardiness irritates me
greatly. I suspect he knows it.

On the phone, he had insisted that my constant mistrust of
Darko is unfounded, that the haunting of the Foggy Bottom
house was surely nothing to do with him, and the
Chairman himself could explain why. But it can

be no coincidence that Darko and I were both fostered by Jean, and are both now members of SPRUNG and rivals to become Chief Ghostkeeper. The Chairman took me to live with the Beaches – did he do the same for Darko? Why didn't anyone ever tell me?

"This is a nice place, Ag. Try something new." The Chairman ordered a salad – beetroot and goat's cheese – while I ordered a Salad Niçoise, a French dish made with eggs, olives, potatoes, tomatoes, anchovies, and tuna (the Chairman smiled approvingly), though I asked the waitress to hold the eggs, olives, potatoes, tomatoes, and anchovies.

"So just the tuna, then?"

"Yes, please. And could you serve it between two pieces of bread?"

It was a really good salad. I ate while the Chairman talked.

THE SALAD WAS DELICIOUS...

1:12 p.m.

"Your foster mother was, let's say, a talent scout for SPRUNG. She spotted Darko when he was very young. So clever!" The Chairman eats with gusto, waving his cutlery around between bites. My eyes follow the line of his fork and stops at his glass of wine. A frosted, tiny, chubby-cheeked smile appears in moisture round the rim.

The Chairman watches me closely, chewing. "Ag?" His mouth is full.

I close my eyes and open them. The face is gone. I sneeze with enough force to shake the table. My skull feels full of fog.

I shake my head. "But you took Darko to her, like me!" I say.

"No, no. You were different. I always knew with you. Darko was entirely Jean's discovery. That boy turned Jean's life inside out!

He didn't stay long before we found him a new family in Europe."

"In that case, I have to contact Darko, and find out what he may know about the Phantasmist up there, what's he's hiding."

"Absolutely not. I forbid it. The fewer of us who know what you have found at that Foggy Bottom house the better."

I chew my sandwich methodically. He mistakes my silence for anger and speaks consolingly, "Ag, I know this has to be hard for you. But I think I can

ELLIE—
THE GIRL
I NEVER
KNEW

help you with this case - and at the same time show you why Darko can't be behind this. You see, Jean had a child of her own - a child I doubt Darko knew about. Ellie. Tragically, she ran away in her teens, then disappeared. It was never really clear. I believe that's why Jean took to foster care as much as she did."

"Jean never mentioned her."

The Chairman pulls an envelope from his jacket pocket.

"No. I'm not surprised. Jean never talked about Ellie at all . . . once we knew she was truly gone. Her husband, Russell, could barely stand being in the house from then on, and eventually he just upped and left. You remember that, I'm sure."

"I do, but I assumed he left because of me."

The Chairman shakes his head. "Everything doesn't revolve around you, Ag."

He pulls a small photograph from the envelope. The surface is creased and worn, and tattered slightly at the edges. The picture is of a young girl - with wide-set eyes and dark hair like mine. It looks like she's been swimming.

"I always thought you reminded Jean of Ellie," the Chairman smiles kindly. "You can see what's happening now, Ag, I'm sure. Ellie's spirit wants to take back her birthright as Jean's child. She's jealous of you. Your inheritance of the house triggered the flood."

I take a sip of water. "I don't even want the house!"

"I very much doubt Ellie does either. But your fate and hers are twinned somehow. I think you - not Darko, not me - are the only one who can help Ellie's spirit find its path. Jean always said you were two halves of a whole."

The Chairman pushes the photograph into my hand with a final word:

"And keep Darko out of it."

END OF LOG

I decided this wasn't the time to mention I'd already written to Darko. Besides, I couldn't stop staring at the photograph of Ellie. Her face was so familiar, like looking into a mirror. What was it the Chairman said? Two halves of a whole.

PHANTASMIST

GHOSTKEEPER'S FINAL CASE OBSERVATIONS:

- The Chairman says it must be my destiny to collect the Spectral Flush and become Chief. Otherwise, why would I have found such a rare ghost hanging around my childhood home?
- I don't believe in destiny or luck — things happen because you make them happen, or someone else does.
- My specs have stopped misting up, which is making it easier to see things clearly.
- I miss Jean. I will be alone next Thanksgiving. Maybe I can spend it with Lily Zhang — if I can find her.

ECTO-ENERGY TYPE
KINTERGEIST

CASE FILE

#ToastGhost

CASE FILE: 24999
GHOSTKEEPER: Agamemnon White
LOCATION: Amsterdam, Holland
PRELIMINARY OUTLINE: 10 April

Well, that lunch with Agamemnon was certainly awkward. I'd known the day would come, so naturally was ready with the explanation he needed to hear.

Of course, I could have told Ag the truth. He'd been haunted by this same Phantasmist ghost ever since I first met him! Ag should have known himself – all those faces in liquids, condensation, and the mist on his specs. That ghost was literally right in front of him all the time! But like I said, Ag didn't pay much attention to his own self. If he had, it would have been as clear to him as it was to me that the sudden flooding at Foggy Bottom wasn't a hostile act, but a protective one.

Regardless, he'd caught the ghost he was after. And that would help him to win the race for Chief Ghostkeeper – just as I hoped he would. So, I didn't tell him the truth . . . about his sister . . . It's more interesting this way, don't you agree?

Meanwhile, it's time you know more about Darko Mantich. Born during the Yugoslav war in the 1990s, the weight of the dead traveled with Darko as a young orphan refugee. By the time Jean Beach spotted his unique capabilities, his mistrust of the world was already ingrained. Darko had learned to trust only what he could see for himself – and mistrust everything else.

Darko masked this mistrust of the world with a cheerful charm that attracted many into his orbit. Darko's personality burns bright and many have felt the heat of the flame, for better or worse. It is a fine line between the rascal and the rogue, the prankster and the bully, or, indeed, the keeper and the hunter. Helani Hekili would have seen herself in Darko and conversely Darko reminds me of Helani. And Helani reminds me of ghouls. Therefore: Darko makes me uncomfortable and I must protect my legacy.

SPRUNG has evolved, just as society has changed. New leaders, new tools, new techniques. Soon it will be my turn to move on, and I must speed up the pace of change while I still can.

You must hurry. I can feel my time is short and your mission is still far from complete.

Additional notes:

INTRODUCTION TO CASE ELEMENTS AND ODDITIES

- Toasters all around the globe have suddenly been exhibiting paranormal interference.
- The first machine designed to slice bread was invented in 1912, and created the need for a machine that could toast the slices.
- Inventors raced to patent the first electric toaster. It seems not everyone was happy with the outcome.

Personally, I much prefer tuna fish on toast than on bread.

SUSPECTED INSTIGATING INCIDENT OR TRIGGER FOR EVENTS UNKNOWN

Shortly after the demise of cult rock star Hot T, an unusual image went viral online. Hot T's face had spontaneously appeared on a piece of toast. There wasn't just one piece of toast with Hot T's image burned into it, but a vast number around the world. And nearly every single one of them was now being shared on social media with the hashtag #ToastGhost. This was normally a phenomenon reserved for religious icons like Buddha and Mother Teresa, so this was certainly newsworthy, if somewhat ridiculous.

There was just one problem. A problem I spotted immediately. The image on the toast wasn't Hot T . . . It was SPRUNG's Head of Ghostkeeping for the Eastern Region, Darko Mantich!

DARKO MANTICH ON TOAST

Darko did not respond well to my assertion that he was in some way responsible for this unexpected apparition. In his defence, there were soon more and more reportings of various faces appearing on toast.

Darko posted an image on his own feed, directing the post at me with the caption: "Burned!"

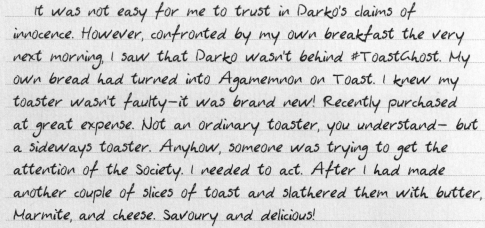

PRELIMINARY OUTLINE OF ODD, WEIRD, AND
OTHERWISE GHOSTLY BEHAVIOR

#toastghost

It was not easy for me to trust in Darko's claims of innocence. However, confronted by my own breakfast the very next morning, I saw that Darko wasn't behind #ToastGhost. My own bread had turned into Agamemnon on Toast. I knew my toaster wasn't faulty—it was brand new! Recently purchased at great expense. Not an ordinary toaster, you understand— but a sideways toaster. Anyhow, someone was trying to get the attention of the Society. I needed to act. After I had made another couple of slices of toast and slathered them with butter, Marmite, and cheese. Savoury and delicious!

I had owned a traditional pop-up toaster for years, a Toastfaster 3000, I believe. But I happened to see a British TV show called The Saucy Chef a couple of years ago, in which the Saucy Chef himself recommended turning your toaster on its side to make melted cheese on toast. Given my enjoyment of a tuna melt as an alternative to my regular tuna sandwich, I thought this might work for me, until I read that the London fire brigade had repeatedly been called out to deal with fires started by the Saucy's Chef's fans foolishly following his advice. I wondered whether #ToastGhost might have been a

AG ON TOAST - TASTED PERFECTLY
NORMAL WITH MARMITE AND CHEESE.

victim of these breakfast blazes, but there appeared to be no record of any loss of life in the fires.

So I began to investigate my new Dutch toaster instead - the Sideloader Mark 2, made by a company in Amsterdam called Bergkamp and Cruyff. Had their new product triggered some ecto-response from beyond the grave?

 GHOSTKEEPER'S LOG - GHOSTKEEPER'S LOG - GHOSTKEEPER'S LOG

15 April
Amsterdam, Holland, Europe
8:32 a.m.
I catch a flight overseas and head to the toaster offices of Bergkamp and Cruyff, on the Grimburgwal, a small canal and street in the center of Amsterdam. Since I arrive before the offices are open, I find a table at the restaurant next door.

Despite sharing the premises with a toaster manufacturer, the restaurant is a pancake house and doesn't even serve toast. There are 103 teapots dangling from the ceiling and 25 pancake options on the menu. But none are served with tuna, which is unfortunate. The place is tiny and I am the only customer, which means that the two proprietors smile at me and nod encouragingly as I pick at the speck on my plate. Apparently 'speck' is Dutch for bacon, but I'm no bacon expert, so I can't be sure.

NOT A VERY PRACTICAL USE OF TEAPOTS

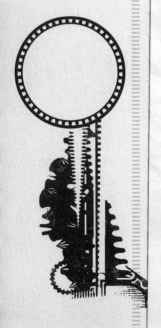

9:01 a.m.

I am relieved to leave the restaurant. Jonas Cruyff greets me at the office door, shaking my hand even as he turns smoothly to point out the small toaster workshop where his company designs its products.

"In Dutch we call a toaster a Broodrooster, because it is used to make 'geroosterd brood,'" Cruyff explains enigmatically. Literal translation? This is a Bread Roaster we use to make Roasted Bread (otherwise known as Toast!). "And this research lab is where the magic happens . . ." The room he leads me to is not in fact magical - it's mechanical, a workshop full of machines under construction. Here he introduces me to a young woman with a mound of red hair piled on her head and goggles partially obscuring her freckled face. "This is our resident genius—Ann Schmetterling. I'll let her show you around."

Ann greets me warmly enough, but as soon as Cruyff is gone, her manner changes completely. She pulls her goggles up on to her forehead and fixes me with a glare of her piercing green eyes, reminding me briefly of *The Girl with the Fan*. "I know why you're here. You're looking for my grandfather's ghost."

It appears Ann Schmetterling has Ecto-Sense.

The Schmetterling Residence

It turns out Ann's grandfather, Hans Schmetterling, was an inventor. But more than this, he was a complete and utter failure. Ann lives in the family home, a rambling flat whose main feature is a ramshackle collection of her grandfather's mementos and inventions. Lily Zhang would not feel out of place

THE "TIPPER"

THE "FLOPPER"

THE "SWEETHEART"

here, surrounded by bizarre and sometimes beautiful machines in various stages of construction. The most extraordinary thing about them, according to Ann, is that absolutely none of them work.

"Honestly, my grandfather's imagination was greater than his capability to actually make things," Ann explained. "It didn't help that he was dyslexic and regularly reversed the sequence of elements by mistake. But his toaster was supposed to be different." Ann sighed. "The toaster was going to change everything."

Although people have been toasting bread since Roman times, it wasn't until someone invented a machine to make evenly sliced bread in the 1900s that the toaster battle really began, led by inventors across the globe, each hoping to make burned toast a thing of the past.

There were many early efforts, named for their key function—the Flopper, the Swinger, the Percher, the Tipper. Each was designed with a different mechanism for loading the bread toward the heating element. But all required a person first toast on one side and then the other. How annoying!

NO IDEA WHY THIS FAILED...

During World War One, Ann's grandfather distracted himself from the unpleasantness of the trenches with memories of his mother's kitchen and her main speciality: breakfast. Hans Schmetterling imagined a better toaster, one that would toast both sides at once and automatically eject the toast when ready. Since this was a good distraction from actually fighting, Hans survived the war. After the war, he drew up plans for his new invention, which he described as a side-loading toaster, sensibly named the Sideloader. He sent his plans to the rich friend of a friend in New York, a man who made a business of financing inventions.

Unfortunately for Hans, he wasn't alone in his bread-based ambition. An American named Charles Strite was working

HANS SCHMETTERLING
ON A BAD HAIR DAY

on a similar idea. And, unlike Hans's prototype, the American's toaster worked. Every time. Thanks in part to its New York financier, Charles patented his concept in 1919 and by the early 1920s his new invention took American breakfast tables by storm. His 'pop-up' toaster remains the model for almost every toaster in the world.

For years, Hans wandered the house, muttering "Pop-up . . . Pop-up", poring over his blueprints, hoping to find the answer to his failing. But he never did.

6:00 p.m.

"I loved looking at my grandfather's blueprints as a child - how I wished I could create with him! But it wasn't until after I studied electrical engineering at college that I found some discrepancies in his plans.

By then, he had died. I couldn't find the blueprints, just his sketches and diagrams. So I created a new set of blueprints myself from his notes - and that's the basis for the Cruyff and Bergkamp toaster you now own."

Ann stares at Hans's portrait above the fireplace.

"I thought it would make my grandfather happy. But it didn't. It made him crazy. If my toaster works now, why didn't his then?"

I made a mental note to recommend Ann Schmetterling to my colleagues in SPRUNG recruitment. She not only has the ability to sense ecto-presence as she had with her grandfather's troubled spirit, but her technical skills might make her a perfect understudy for Lily Zhang one day.

16 April
Amsterdam, Holland, Europe

Additional notes:

6:06 a.m.

I watch the sunrise in Vondelpark, in the centre of
Amsterdam. Jet lag has confused my sleep cycles.
When I use my handkerchief to wipe the dew off the
park bench, it occurs to me that I haven't sneezed
in weeks.

Ann Schmetterling let me take scans of her
father's papers with me, and I'm examining
them in the dawning sunlight when a shadow
passes across the pages. I see the cane
first, then the cape.

"It's been far too long, Agamemnon," says
Darko Mantich.

7:15 a.m.

"I got your telegram."

We are in a coffee shop near the park.
When our food arrives, Darko instantly
Instagrams it.

"Why do you do that, Darko? You really are
an egomaniac! Do you honestly think people
care what you are having for breakfast?"

I TOOK A PHOTO OF DARKO
TAKING A PHOTO OF HIS COFFEE.

Darko looks down at my creamed tuna.

"At least my breakfast won't scare them."

We stare at each other. Darko looks away. I win.

"I do it for my own protection. I do it so people
know where I am and what I'm doing. If I stop
posting suddenly, if I disappear, people will
notice. You, on the other hand, could disappear and
nobody would have a clue."

Darko takes a large bite of fried egg. "And, yes,
I'm also an egg-omaniac!"

Darko laughs at either his egg or his joke. I'm not
sure which.

"Why would you disappear? Why would I?"

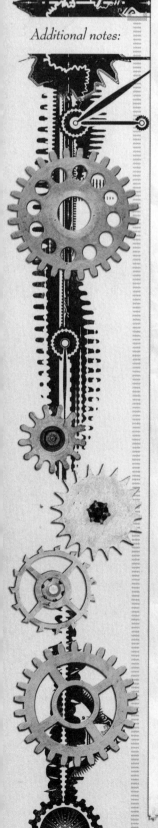

"My dear Agamemnon, have you not noticed that things are a bit strange these days?"

"Of course they're strange. We are part of a secret society that pursues ghosts. Everything we do is strange."

"Not so strange that our Chief Ghostkeeper should drop dead two days after reaching out to Helani Hekili."

"Helani Hekili? Don't be ridiculous. She's long gone."

"She was gone. Not anymore. I've met her. The day after Martin McKoken contacted her. Do you know what Helani Hekili told me? That I should resign at once, leave SPRUNG for good, and trust no one that asks me to collect ghosts if I don't want to wind up a ghoul. The next morning, Martin McKoken was dead. I plan to follow her advice. I strongly recommend you do the same."

I take in what Darko has just said. And then I take a bite of toast. "I don't believe you," I say finally. "You're just trying to confuse me."

"You want proof? Take your Ghost-o-Matic and look at the 'Five Founders' page at the front of the Journal." Darko reaches for my Journal, but I pull it away.

"You're crazy."

"Why? Because I still believe in the existence of ghouls? And believe Helani Hekili is right when she says there's a ghoul in SPRUNG? Or because I don't believe your precious Chairman when he claims they are just a fairytale to scare children with?"

"You're unbelievable, Darko. You want ghouls to be real, don't you?"

Darko looks surprised for once. "Maybe I do, Ag. At least then things might make some sense. Because at the moment things don't add up at SPRUNG."

"I'm not going to listen to you. You just want to be made Chief Ghostkeeper ahead of me."

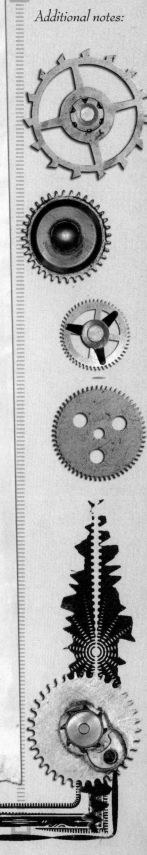

Darko gives me a look he intends to be withering. "Is that so?"

It is rather withering. I feel quite withered.

"I don't want to talk to you," I say. "I have work to do." I pull out Hans Schmetterling's papers and loudly say nothing.

"You should listen to me, Ag. Besides, you do want to talk to me. That's what you said in your telegram anyway. Tell me about Jean Beach."

He's right. I tell Darko what had happened at the Foggy Bottom Canyon house after Jean died: the flooding and the papers. I share what the Chairman told me about Jean's daughter. And I ask him why he'd never told me that he'd been raised by Jean, too.

"You never asked," he says. "As for Samantha, I'd have thought Jean would have told you all about her."

"Who's Samantha?"

"The person we're talking about, dumb-dumb! Jean and Russell's daughter. The Chairman didn't tell you? She was named after Russell's father, Sam. But she died as a baby."

"That's not right. Her name was Ellie and she was a teenager when she disappeared. I've seen her picture."

"I should know. I went to live with them right after it all happened. I was the first of Jean's collection. Her living dolls. All us foster kids, we were all replacements for Samantha. Though I think she took me in at first because she thought I could bring back Samantha's spirit. You would have thought she'd be happy when I told her that Samantha's spirit had gone to rest and that there was nothing I could - or needed - to do. She wouldn't believe me."

"That's because you were wrong."

"Now you're being ridiculous!"

"You were wrong. I caught her spirit. She's in my journal right now."

Darko reached out an open-palmed hand. "Show me."

"I'm not opening my journal in here! All my ghosts might get loose."

Darko gave me that withering look again.

"Ag, I don't know whose ghost you have in that journal and I'm not sure I should care. But it's not Jean Beach's daughter. Ask Russell - if you can find him. Her name wasn't Ellie, she wasn't a restless spirit and she isn't in your book. Somebody's playing games with you. Why don't you just hand over the journal and we'll see?"

"You're the one playing games, Darko. You have been since you walked in here."

Faster than I expect, Darko grabs for my journal. I slam my hand on it just as he pulls the book toward him. He is determined. And strong. The journal slips from my grasp.

ALL THAT'S LEFT
OF DARKO

A piece of toast hits Darko square in the face. In his surprise he lets go of the book. Another piece of toast flies past my nose. Suddenly toast is flying in all directions around the coffee shop. The kinetic energy of a powerful Kintergeist spirit operating at full force. The chef runs out from behind the counter, a tornado of geroosterd brood pursuing him. It sounds like someone is yelling though a wind tunnel: "Pop-up! Pop-up! Pop-up!"

And then it all stops.

And Darko Mantich is gone.

17 April
Somewhere over the Atlantic Ocean
12:15 p.m.

Normally I don't like flying.
My congested sinuses make the changes in air
pressure painful, keeping me from sleep. But for
the first time I can remember, my sinuses are fine.
I'm able to enjoy the flight - counting the number
of peanuts in each individual packet: 32, then 29,
33 . . . until I fall asleep.

A dream. Darko is there, wearing his cape. Except
it's not Darko, it's Hot T, the rock star, and
he's eating toast. And there's an alarm ringing.
It's the SPRUNG Ghost-o-
Matic ghoul alert. I try to
switch it off but it won't
stop . . .

The flight attendant shakes
me awake. In my sleep, I've
been repeatedly pressing
the call button by my seat.
We are commencing our
descent to New York's John
F. Kennedy airport.

NEW YORK - 115,758,932 WINDOWS
THAT I CAN SEE.

18 April
New York, NY, USA
8:00 a.m.

I placed a phone call to Lily Zhang to tell her about Ann
Schmetterling's Ecto-Sense and technology skills. Lily's response
was puzzling:
    "I'm not here to help you get a ghoul, friend!" she barked.
Perhaps she said 'girlfriend.' The connection was terrible, so I
wasn't sure.
    Darko's talk about ghouls was messing with my head.

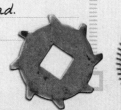

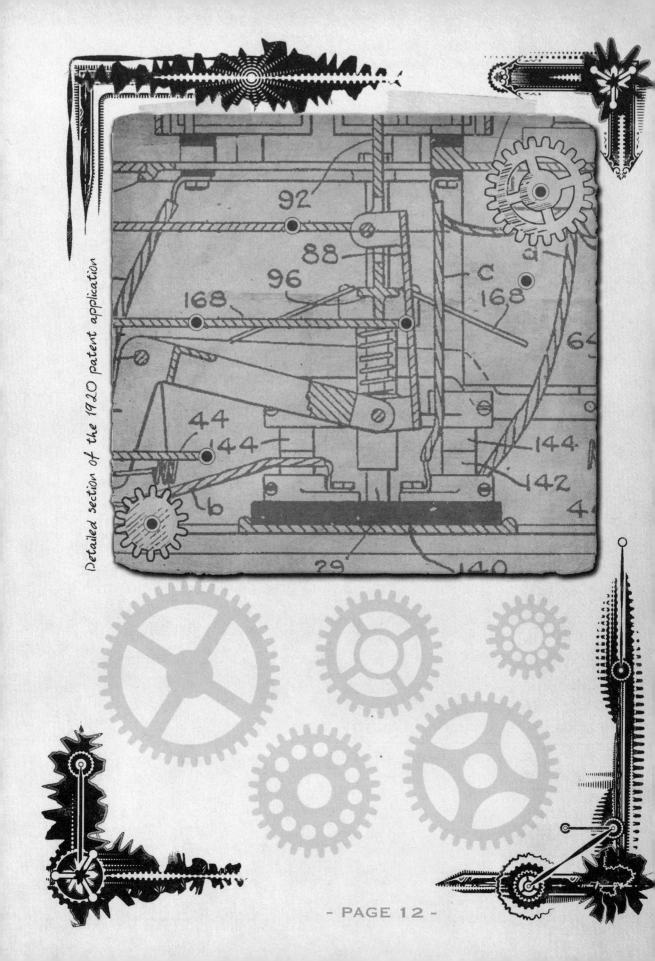

Detailed section of the 1920 patent application

<u>10.00 a.m.</u>

I am at the offices of Dean and Danziger, a
venture capital firm. Richard Danziger, one of
the partners, greets me. I see his nose before I
spot the rest of his face - to be
accurate, his nose is his face. But
he is amiable and keen to help.
It was his father, Harry Danziger,
who was approached by the friend
of Hans Schmetterling in the 1920s,
soliciting for financial support for
Hans's Sideloader toaster.

"My father was fascinated by
technology—he was trained as an
engineer before the war and he
liked a nice piece of toast. So he
was intrigued by the Schmetterling
design. But he'd also been contacted
by Charles Strite, who had patented
his own pop-up toaster. So my father
had both machines built and tested - a toast-off,
if you will. Sadly, the Schmetterling Sideloader
failed to function."

I ask how it was possible to prototype the designs
without the inventors' help. Couldn't someone have
assembled the Sideloader incorrectly?

Danziger shakes his head vigorously. The work had
been done to the precise specifications of the
blueprints Schmetterling had sent from Amsterdam.
To prove his point, Danziger produces a set of
blueprints from an ancient folder.

I hold the document next to the scan of the
blueprint I received from Ann at her home in
Holland. On a light box, the two sets align
perfectly. Except in the cog mechanism. Here, at
last, was the sad proof : Ann and Hans had drawn up
completely different configurations for the cogs.

The design for Hans Schmetterling's Sideloader
toaster sits illuminated on the light box, a
ghost of the invention that never quite worked.
I switch off the light and thank Mr Danziger for
his time. The cogs continue to glow in the darkened
room, calling out to the Kintergeist spirit of
their inventor.

END OF LOG

HARRY
DANZIGER
WAS A
GADGET
BUFF

RICHARD
DANZIGER'S
NOSE
PRECEDED
HIM INTO
THE ROOM

KINTERGEIST

GHOSTKEEPER'S FINAL CASE OBSERVATIONS:

- Four ecto-energy types collected now - that's very close to five. But I'm not certain why I'm capturing them anymore.
- Helani Hekili is real. Darko was right about that.
- If Helani met Martin McKoken before he died, was it her bad breath Martin made a note about on his files?
- Does the Chairman know about her? He must. Does he believe she's a ghoul? Is he trying to protect me?

Yes, Ag met Darko Mantich in Amsterdam, and now you have, too, through these pages, at least. You will have noticed, as I have, that Darko is a most eccentric character. Perhaps I should have done more to calm the rivalry between Ag and Darko . . . but where's the fun in that? A little competition never hurt anyone and both young men achieved great things in their efforts to outperform the other.

It's worth noting that we at the Society have not heard from Darko since Ag's disappearance. So, why are we not seeking Darko, too? Because the man cannot stop sharing photos of his breakfast, no matter where he is—he eats the strangest things. Could Ag be with him? A good question, but if he is, it wouldn't be willingly. It seems to me that Darko certainly wanted Ag's journal.

And Darko told Ag about Helani Hekili. You'll note that I've made no secret in my notes to you about this troublesome one-time queen of Hawaii or whatever grand title she claimed to have. But perhaps I should have shared more. As you'll no doubt have seen by now, Helani was indeed one of the original founders of SPRUNG. Ag will be disappointed to know that there were in fact six founders, not five. But that changed at the very first full meeting of the group, the meeting where we tested the prototype of Lily Zhang's Ghostkeeper's Journal.

At that time, I was young, rich, engaged to be married . . . and miserable. When I was a child, I had lost my twin sister to scarlet fever. And yet, decades later, I felt as though Millicent was still with me. I needed to speak to her – to make the connection we had, as twins do, one more time before marrying. So I left Harvard to study reincarnation in Egypt, tried every spiritualist I could find, studied the occult, but all was wasted time and money. Until I met Madame D'Olivera Balding.

She could sense Millicent's presence at once. She opened my eyes to the energies I could feel around me – and with her guidance, I assembled the team we now know as SPRUNG's founders. The remarkable Martin McKoken, the most effective analyst of ecto-impulses I'd ever seen. Nettie Dahl, who strangely had no Ecto-Sense herself, but could channel the vision through contact with others – a powerful tool for cataloguing apparitions. And, of course, the enigmatic Lily Zhang, master of disguise and one time ophthalmologist who connected Madame D'Olivera Balding's theories into the most extraordinary mechanisms, allowing us to capture ghosts and hold their energy to perform a Resolution.

And then, my great mistake – Helani Hekili. She was known as a skeptic, a woman with both great power and great caution. She came to me with warnings about ghouls and the harm a ghoul could achieve with the full energy spectrum. I knew we were exploring terra incognita and felt Helani's strengths would protect us from whatever we might encounter. Madame D'Olivera Balding did not agree. I should have listened to her.

On the night we finally tested what we had designed, SPRUNG was truly born. We used the ghosts that I had collected in Lily's prototype journal and Lily's first SPRUNG Ghost-o-Matic device, made from watch parts, gemstones, and cataracts from human eyes. It was magnificent!

SPRUNG was born, but at what cost? The death of Madame D'Olivera Balding, thanks to the crazed imaginings of Helani Hekili. She claimed to have slain the ghoul. And what had she really achieved? To be kind, she'd created such a fearful frenzy that an old woman was overcome. But I came to believe she intended to accomplish exactly what she did – she made a very old woman die of fright. I thought then Martin was right to banish – instead of destroy – Helani Hekili. But now I wonder whether I've put all of SPRUNG in danger with my former leniency.

There would be no more Ghoulhunting at SPRUNG. We all saw what Helani's ghoul paranoia could do to harm us. We carried on with Madame D'Olivera Balding's plan, as I believe she would have wanted. The Journal worked, again and again. The remaining founders, like me, have lived to extreme old age, enabled by the ecto-energy surrounding us through our work.

But now, suddenly, Martin McKoken is gone . . . And Ag is missing. And Helani Hekili is back. I am old but I am not afraid. I'm angry. And Darko should be, too. I hope it's not too late for him.

I don't want to unduly influence your path, but I'd watch out for any sign of Darko's influence on future events – keeping him at a distance may help you solve this mystery for us and bring Ag safely home.

As the saying goes, "Clean gloves hide dirty hands."

SURPRISE!

HAPPY BIRTHDAY, JEAN!

wish you were still here . . .

Jean loved surprise birthday parties. This proved trickier and trickier over the years, as she was always expecting the surprise. Jean left strict instructions that she didn't want a formal funeral, so I figured I'd throw her one last surprise birthday party, even if she couldn't attend.

She'd certainly have been surprised by how many people showed up for this final party – other foster parents, officials from the county's child services, my fellow foster kids of course (though not Darko – he sent a huge bouquet of white flowers with a black bow, as if this was Dracula's wedding). Even though the Canyon house was largely cleared out by now, the rooms were small and the downstairs was jammed with people. Neighbours had shown up too, including one who brought a present, perhaps unaware that Jean had passed. There were also current and former SPRUNG operatives, many more than I was aware Jean knew.

I asked the Chairman about them. "They didn't all come for Jean, Ag - they came for you. After all, SPRUNG is your family now."

Another surprise? The Chairman had arrived with Nettie Dahl, SPRUNG's Astro-Philosopher and Chief Archivist. I'd never paid attention to the rumours about the two of them - that they were more than co-founders and colleagues - and perhaps that's why it was so unusual to see them together in public. Nettie had always been cold toward me - I assumed I had done something to offend her (apparently I do that sometimes) but in any event I found the way she stared at me disconcerting, so I was happy to keep my distance.

I busied myself by making sure everything was arranged as Jean would have wanted. She liked a simple surprise party—we all yell "SURPRISE" (generally just me), sing "Happy Birthday," then candles and cake. I wasn't really sure how old she would have been, so I put five candles on the cake. I think she'd have liked that—if she didn't, she never said so, as I did it every year.

People kept coming over to tell me they could feel Jean's spirit with us, but that was ridiculous - I felt nothing. And of course I'd also used SPRUNG technology to confirm that. There was no trace of Jean's ecto-energy or her spirit - only its absence. Which was, in my mind, the hard part.

Also absent was Russell Beach, Jean's former husband. I'd tried to spread the word about the party in the hope that it might reach Russell, but I wasn't surprised he hadn't made it. And Lily Zhang had sent a cryptic two-word message explaining her own absence - "Sorry - engaged!".

But I was surprised when the Chairman stood up and cleared his throat theatrically to make a speech. This was not part of the party plan. Jean and I did not like changes. I quickly moved to a sofa at the back of the room, out of the way. So I was even more surprised - shocked actually - when Nettie Dahl sat down next to me and offered me a breath mint from a small enameled tin she kept in her purse.

"I'm Jeremiah Goodrough, and on behalf of Jean and her family, I'd like to thank you all for coming," the Chairman began. I could barely

SPRUNG ECTO-PRINTING IN JEAN'S
FAVORITE COLORS ... SHE'D LOVE IT!

listen to what followed. I was infuriated—I had planned the party after all, and it was time to sing "Happy Birthday", not make long-winded speeches about the past. I was vaguely aware of Nettie beside me, her minty breath and her fingers resting on my arm. But suddenly, I felt a sharp pain in my hand. Nettie Dahl hadn't just touched me, she'd grabbed my hand around the knuckles, then squeezed with surprising force. She was whispering excitedly in my ear, "Do you see? Do you SEE!"

Honestly, I didn't see anything. I followed Nettie's eyeline, fixed on Jeremiah, who just continued to waffle away, oblivious. "The Phantasmist! Right there above Jeremiah's head. Just like the one the night Madame D'Olivera Balding died . . ."

"I don't see it," I said, because I didn't.

"But you must!" she protested, turning toward me. Her eyes were ecstatically wide, as if she'd seen a ghost. Of course, she thought she had. "You know I can only see ecto-energy through one of you with the Sense . . ." And then doubt came into her expression. "But you don't see it. Of course you don't . . ." Her voice trailed off as she let go of my hands. "Excuse me." She leapt up and ran from the room.

I found her outside. Her disconcerting stare was back. "I am sorry. I was overcome by the event. So many memories. I'm imagining things." She shot me a final wild-eyed glare. And with that, she turned on her heel and marched off, leaving the party behind.

The surprises weren't done with me yet. I went back inside as the Chairman was winding up his speech. He finished by asking for a moment of silence in memory of Jean. And that's when it happened. I sneezed. I sneezed again. Suddenly I couldn't stop sneezing. I reached into my pocket for my handkerchief - the purple one with the blue polka dots - and my hand found instead a piece of paper. I blew my nose anyway, and only later discovered I had just made a mess all over the death certificate of Madame D'Olivera Balding.

And why was I suddenly sneezing again?

S.P.R.U.N.G.

POST-MORTEM, PRE-SPIRITUS ASSESSMENT
CONFIDENTIAL

DATE: 15 NOVEMBER, 1917   **CONDUCTED BY:** NETTIE DAHL

DECEASED: MADAME D'OLIVERA BALDING

SEX: FEMALE   **AGE:** 92   **CAUSE OF DEATH:** HEART FAILURE

NOTES:

The deceased appears to have been in failing health, with multiple
ailments that would in time have led to death. However, the immediate
cause appears to have been extreme shock based on her circumstances at
the time of her demise.

ECTO-ENERGIES OR OTHER PARANORMAL MANIFESTATIONS:

While those SPRUNG operatives present on the night of her death had
been convinced by Ghosthunter Helani Hekili that the subject might be
possessed by a dangerous GHOUL (Ghoulius periculus), our examination
revealed no conclusive evidence to support this belief. Any paranormal
manifestations witnessed at the séance appear to have resulted from
use of the prototype SPRUNG journal, not the medium Mme D'Olivera
Balding. Her body is deceased and the spirit it contained, if any,
appears to have made a direct transition to rest.

CONCLUSION:

SPRUNG founders must reconsider methodology around, or even the
existence of the major GHOUL or indeed any other kind of GHOUL, based
on this massive failure of both the subject's heart and the Society's
objectives. I recommend the suspension of GHOST AND GHOUL HUNTING
METHODOLOGY indefinitely.

*This "postmortem" report seems to have been a whitewash of the
facts - designed to justify pushing Helani Hekili away from SPRUNG.
Did the author of the report do this deliberately or was she
manipulated? Did the other founders know enough about their new
technology to understand what they had enabled with their work?
If the prototype journal used contained a Spectral Flush of ecto-energy,
a ghoul could have possessed any one of those present . . .*

ECTO-ENERGY TYPE
PHANTASMIST

CASE FILE

Runaway, part 2

CASE FILE:	24852-2
GHOSTKEEPER:	Agamemnon White
LOCATION:	California & Mexico
PRELIMINARY OUTLINE:	23 April

So there are "rumours" about myself and my dear old friend Nettie Dahl. I suppose a secret society must have its secrets. But it's no secret that Nettie and I have been close for many years. Nettie helped me through the loss of my twin sister, Millicent, to whom I was devoted, and in many ways, Nettie became as devoted to me. At one time we were betrothed to be married, but all that changed after the night Madame D'Olivera Balding died.

It was Nettie who introduced me – introduced all of us – to Madame D'Olivera Balding over a century ago, so I suppose you could say that the existence of SPRUNG is as much the result of Nettie's introduction as it was inspired by Madame D'Olivera and her extraordinary spirit-investigation techniques.

Madame D'Olivera guided me to reach out to my sister's ghost and help her find peace. For that I will always be grateful. But Madame D'Olivera was easily misunderstood – her behaviour was strange and her motives obscure. It led to unfortunate events. And Nettie is confused. The last time she saw a Phantasmist was the night of my sister Millicent's séance. The night Helani Hekili accused Madame D'Olivera Balding of being a ghoul. The night she died. Nettie didn't know about Ag's Phantasmist until tonight.

Ag was also growing more aware of the unfortunate events that night so long ago, just as you are now. It appears he was growing confused, unclear, un-Ag if I may say so, and it makes me worry more and more about his fate. Please hurry.

INTRODUCTION TO CASE ELEMENTS AND ODDITIES

• **This case is not officially assigned**

- Now that Jean is gone, SPRUNG really is my only family.
- If the Chairman needs my help, I must be there for him. He has always been there for me.
- So should I tell him about Nettie Dahl? Her strange behaviour? Her breath? Does he already know?
- Only the Toxigon is needed now to complete the Spectral Flush. I will complete this journal soon. Why does it scare me?

INITIAL OUTLINE OF ODD, WEIRD, AND OTHERWISE GHOSTLY BEHAVIOR

23 April
 Santa Monica, CA

I had started sneezing again at Jean's party at the house in the Canyon. I thought it was psychological, being back where I grew up. It hadn't stopped when I left, however. Fortunately, I was now equipped with the red handkerchief with the yellow polka dots, so it was not a hygiene crisis. It was, however, a Tuesday.

   I needed to find a Toxigon that could be captured safely, without exposing myself to radiation. Toxigons are notorious for haunting nuclear reactor cores – for example, there's a famous one at the old Dearborn State University decommissioned research reactor. No Ghostkeeper has ever attempted its capture, as it would require exposure to deadly gamma rays. The first principle of ghostkeeping is to help the troubled dead, not become one of them.

Additional notes:

In search of alternatives, I was reviewing the notes in my Ghostkeeper's Journal and Field Guide while traveling back to Santa Monica along the Pacific Coast Highway. I was alone in the bus, so I saw no risk in opening the journal. But to my horror, I discovered that the Phantasmist - the spirit of Ellie,

Jean Beach's lost child - was gone. I immediately tried to lure the spirit back with the photograph the Chairman had given me, but the SPRUNG Ghost-o-Matic Scanner showed no gathering ecto-energy at all. She had vanished, and I couldn't summon her back.

WARM DAY, EMPTY BUS. BUT SOMEHOW THE WINDOWS ARE ALL STEAMED—AND SHE'S GONE FROM THE JOURNAL.

I considered the moment in Amsterdam when Darko had made a grab for the journal. But it seemed impossible he could have caused this - if he had succeeded in opening the book, he would have released all the spirits, not just one.

No, somehow Ellie's ghost had escaped. Phantasmists are extremely rare, in part because they are known to be slippery creatures. Any ghost can slip through your fingers, but the Phantasmist is also exceptionally hard to see, even for the trained eye, unless it wishes to be seen. You feel the presence, but you can't pin it down. That's why we call them Runaways.

If the lure no longer drew El back, it meant that I had somehow failed to understand the object's meaning—the hold would only be as strong as the power of the image to appease the troubled part of her being. I would need to understand more to capture her again. I would need to find Jean's ex-husband, Russell Beach.

When I hurried home to get a change of handkerchief before starting my search, I found another example of someone seeming to direct my next move. Was it a coincidence? Or something more sinister?

PUERTO ESCONDIDO, OAX.

THERE WAS A POSTCARD FROM RUSSELL BEACH ASKING ME TO COME OVER TO SEE HIM… IN MEXICO.

 GHOSTKEEPER'S LOG - GHOSTKEEPER'S LOG - GHOSTKEEPER'S LOG

25 April
Puerto Escondido, Mexico
4.00 p.m.

The FBB Hotel and Café is more like a hippy commune than an international travel destination. Long-haired surfers in baggy shorts and flip-flops wander about sipping smoothies, while the proprietor, his shaggy beard and old-school Wayfarer shades making him a dead ringer for the Dude in a movie I once saw, holds court at a table under a palm tree.

This seems an unlikely place to find Russell Beach. The man I knew when I was child was as buttoned-up as they come - quite literally. I believe he even owned a pair of button-down underpants. So, when I hear someone call my name and I realize it's the Dude . . . I'm amazed. Russell stands, his beard blowing in the breeze and grins at me, not a button in sight.

MY CABIN WAS NUMBER 5

THERE WERE 5 SURFBOARDS ON THE OPPOSITE WALL. I WAS FEELING LUCKY. I WAS MISTAKEN.

Russell showed me around the FBB Hotel. I should have realized from the initials - they stand for Foggy Bottom Beach - that he was the owner, not just a resident. The hotel was made up of several bungalows around a central courtyard and main house, with a path leading straight down to the stunning white-sand beach.

"Hey, I figured I've been called a Beach all my life," Russell explained as he waved his arm toward the crashing surf. "I might as well have a piece of it."

He showed me to an empty bungalow. "Here you go, number three. My personal favorite."

I hesitated at the door. Russell paused a beat, then smiled broadly.

"My mistake. Your bungalow is just down the way here."

He stopped in front of an identical hut, except this one was number five. Perfect.

Russell told me to make myself at home, clean up from my journey and meet him for dinner. The room inside was shaded and cool, a relief from the extreme

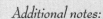

Additional notes:

heat and light outside. Russell stood silhouetted in the doorway.

"I need to ask you some urgent questions, Russell. About Jean and –"

Russell held up a hand to cut me off.

"Agamemnon, I didn't think you'd travel thousands of miles to come and sit on the sand with me. I remember what you like and it isn't relaxing in the sunshine and working on your tan. But I'm glad you're here, and we've got plenty of time. Besides, I've been expecting you."

Those hairs on my neck were at attention again, and I felt that niggling in my stomach.

"Who told you I was coming?"

"No one. It's just that for the last two nights my bedroom has been absolutely freezing, without the air-conditioning switched on. I recognized that feeling. It happened when you first came to live with us. Get some rest." Russell closed the bungalow door, leaving me in the gloom.

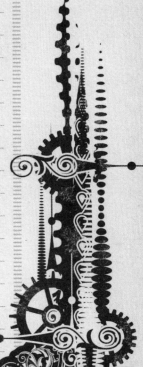

6:15 p.m.

I have been dozing in my room, but awake to hear voices outside, one with a South American accent, the other from the north.

North American: "The surf is awesome here, dude."

South American: "Beeg waves. Beeg, beeg waves."

North American: "You said it, man."

South American: "But not as beeg as in my country. We have super-beeg waves."

Additional notes

North American: "Bigger than here? That's totally loco, dude. Where are you from?"

South American: "I'm from Venezuela. It's thee best surfing . . . thee very best."

North American: "I'm goin', man. I'm goin! Hey, look at that weird dude over by bungalow five!"

South American: "What's hee doing? Is hee deeging?"

North American: "Beats me. Weird."

I lie on the bed for another moment. Bungalow Five? That's my bungalow. I leap up and race to the window - nothing - and then on to the door. No one there, except the two surfers carrying their boards back to the beach.

North American: "So where's Venezuela at, man?"

I NEVER SAW THEIR FACES

I couldn't get back to sleep, so I decided to go for a swim - the beach below the hotel was clearly a surfer haunt, but as the waves weren't rolling in, most of the surfboards were planted in the sand like rows of colorful tombstones. I assumed their owners were taking siestas.

The ocean water was calm, warm, and clear. I let my body rise and fall with the ebb and flow of the tide and closed my eyes, floating in perfect limbo. So I never saw it coming. I felt a crack across my skull and everything went black. When I opened my eyes, there was water in every direction - below me, above me, around me, inside me. My lungs felt like they would burst. I saw a glint of light, a fading glow far above. I was sinking away from it. Bubbles streamed upward as I tumbled deeper down.

The old man who found me on the beach said he saw I was hit by a piece of broken surfboard powered by a breaking wave. The impact must have knocked me out. I instantly sank out of sight. He claimed he saw a hand above the surface for a moment in the distance, but then nothing. Until the water round his ankles began to drain away from the beach, almost pulling him off his feet. A clicking sound as pebbles skittered back on the undertow toward the sea. Then the growing roar of a cresting wave, a fearsome tide, a tower of water and foam that came crashing down onto the beach, leaving me coughing and choking, gasping for air as water spilled from my shivering lungs. I had the very strong feeling that I had been here before.

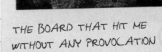

THE BOARD THAT HIT ME
WITHOUT ANY PROVOCATION

<u>8:30 p.m.</u>
By dinnertime, the episode in the waves seems like a bad dream. I can smell the burning coals on the barbecue from across the FBB compound, mixed with the aroma of fresh fish, chillies and spices. I briefly consider bringing my SPRUNG Ghostkeeper's Journal with me after the stranger the surfers spotted, but conclude it will be more secure locked in the room's safe. While the sun is now low in the sky, the atmosphere outside remains sultry and hot, exacerbated by the smoke wafting about. The aromas are so delicious that for once I think I might not miss my usual tuna sandwich.

NOT TUNA :-(

Russell waves to me from his table and I cross the café to join him. Almost before I've sat down, a waiter appears with covered plates he places in front

of us. Russell's cover is whisked away to reveal a whole fresh aromatic snapper. My cover leaves its plate . . . a tuna sandwich on toasted white.

"Your favorite, right?" Russell beams as he starts his fish. "I knew that's what you'd want."

I sigh. He's right. Trying to change my tastes would be foolish. And the tuna sandwich is delicious.

Russell is in his element, greeting guests, offering toasts, even slapping high fives with passing surfers. This man has changed almost beyond recognition. And yet he knows me. In fact, as it turns out, in some ways he knows more about me than I do myself.

"It happened not far from here, you know. The accident." When he sees my puzzled expression, he shakes his head. "Jean never told you, did she?"

"Told me what? About how your daughter died? No. She never even told me you had a kid. I found out from the Chairman."

Now it's Russell's turn to look confused. "Samantha? What do you mean?"

"Not Samantha. Ellie. He gave me her picture." I pass the photo to Russell. He smiles apologetically, and shakes his head. He's lost in memories.

Finally he looks up at me. "I'm sorry, Ag. It seems you have a faulty source."

"How so?"

"Jean and I did have a daughter, but we named her Samantha, after my dad. She died as a baby - it's what tore me and Jean apart. We'd tried for so long, then the

ALOE VERA
CACTUS-
GOOD FOR
MY SUNBURN
ONCE I
UNDERSTOOD
TO CUT IT
OPEN.

joy of her birth and suddenly Sam was gone. I couldn't cope, not like Jean. She threw herself into raising her 'kids', especially you. But I was a wreck inside. I was making things worse. So I came here."

"Then who is the girl in the picture? Do you know her?"

"I don't know her, no. But I do know who she is." Russell takes a sip of his water. "That girl is Electra. Or like you said, Ellie. She was your sister."

It was late when I went back to my bungalow, my mind so wrapped up in all that Russell Beach had told me that I might not have noticed if a circus parade had been making its way past. So I certainly wouldn't have spotted a figure slipping away in the dark. But I could see my bungalow door was open. And so was the room's safe. The Ghostkeeper's Journal was gone.

Russell summoned his staff to search the area, but no intruder was found. Nor was the book. Back in my bungalow, I asked Russell who might have known where he lived, as I was sure no one had followed me to Mexico.

"Well, Jeremiah Goodrough, obviously. And Darko has come down to see me here once or twice. He's quite a good surfer, you know."

"Darko? He's tried to steal my journal before."

Russell shook his head. "Well, he just posted a photo of himself in Tuscany, Italy, eating fresh truffles, so I doubt he could be here too."

"Sounds like everyone knew you was here . . ."

"Nah, just Jeremiah and Darko, that's all."

I was just thinking that, in that case, it must be Darko when Russell continued:

"I suppose there was that woman who was always around your lot.

darkomantich

❤ 💬 ✈ 🔖
Liked by rumpledruss and 15 others
darkomantich Nothing like truffles in Italy
1 HOUR AGO

FRESH TRUFFLES, YES, BUT DARKO'S NOT IN THE PICTURE

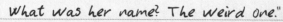

Additional notes:

I KEPT THE TOY BOAT IN FRONT OF MY CANYON BEDROOM WINDOW. NOW I GUESS I KNOW WHY.

What was her name? The weird one."

"That doesn't really narrow it down, Russell. Was it Lily . . . Helani? Nettie?"

"Nettie! That's it. She still sends me Christmas cards. They normally arrive by about March."

Nettie. Who doesn't like me. Who uses strong breath mints. Who works in the archives. Who doesn't have normal Ecto-Sense. Who knew Mme D'Olivera first . . . That Nettie. I decided to get some sleep in what was left of the night and thanked Russell for his help.

"Was the book important?"

"Yes and no," I said as I reached behind the headboard. It would have been, if I hadn't hidden the actual journal out of sight. The one in the safe was empty. My Ghostkeeper's Journal was safe. For now.

On the flight from Mexico back to the States, I had time to think through what Russell had told me about my sister, Ellie, and the rest of my birth family. My father had apparently loved sailing and often took the family out on his sailing boat. You could call it a yacht, but it was one of those old-

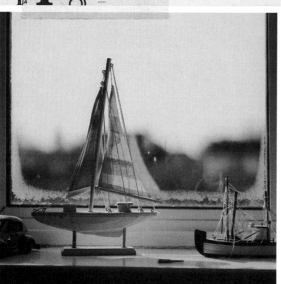

fashioned small boats with an outboard motor available if the wind died, rigged for sailing the way it had been done for centuries, all the way back to the ancient times. My mother was a professor of Latin and Greek. That's why she named her children Agamemnon and Electra.

The storm was sudden and epic, like something out of Homer's Odyssey. The boat foundered in the waters off Baja California. I was just a baby and should have

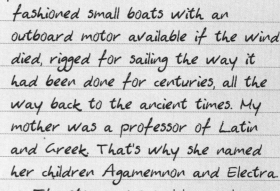

died once my parents vanished in the extreme waves, but my thirteen-year-old sister, Electra, kept me alive. She managed to put me in an old wooden crate that floated past, a container for tins of Smiler's tuna. When I was found washed up on the beach the next morning, barely alive, Ellie was nowhere to be found. Just a sodden note stuffed in my plastic diaper. A few details scrawled on the back of a Smiler's tuna tin label in purple felt-tip pen. Ellie had signed her name for the last time and adorned it with a chubby-cheeked smiley face. A teenage girl's last defiant smile.

I'd tried to obtain a tin of Smiler's tuna before the flight. I felt sure I would need the label to lure Ellie's ghost back into the open. But the company had gone out of business. The odds were turning against me.

    And who was my nemesis now? Was it Darko Mantich, my rival in SPRUNG? Nettie Dahl, who had known Madame D'Olivera and started it all? The mysterious Helani Hekili, who reappeared just as all this talk of ghouls began? Or my mentor, my champion – the man who had lied to me about my sister – Chairman Jeremiah Goodrough? It was time to confront them, one by one. I planned to start with Nettie Dahl. But I hadn't expected the Chairman to be at the airport to meet my flight.

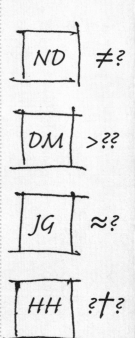

Additional notes:

ND ≠?

DM >??

JG ≈?

HH ?†?

 GHOSTKEEPER'S LOG - GHOSTKEEPER'S LOG - GHOSTKEEPER'S LOG

26 April
7:18 p.m.

 "I'm sorry I lied to you, Ag." The Chairman is, perhaps
 for the first time I can recall, looking every day of his
 immense age.

 "Once I got word you'd gone to see Russell Beach, I knew
 I had to be here to meet your flight and set things
 straight."

Has he always trembled so much? And his breath - has it always smelled so foul?

"I wanted to protect you. I thought I could replace Ellie with Samantha so you wouldn't go through what I went through."

Is that actually a tear on the old man's cragged face? I can't be sure. Perhaps it's a message from the Phantasmist - from Ellie. A warning. I can't tell.

"You may not know that I lost my sister, Millicent, when I was child . . ." Whatever he planned to say next seems to catch in his throat. He looks up at me, as if hoping I'll come to his rescue with words of forgiveness. I don't.

The Chairman places his full weight on the long thin cane in his hands and I can hear his bones groan with the stress. "I spent many years and much of my fortune trying to contact my sister Millicent's spirit. In fact, it was my quest to help her troubled soul that led me to meet all the founders of SPRUNG, as each brought a new skill that might help me achieve my goals."

I imagine that night. The night they all gathered with Madame D'Olivera for Millicent's séance. The origin of SPRUNG.

"Along the path to see my sister once again, I lost sight of how important the living truly can be. I fear I lost a part of myself that night that I can never return to. That's why I chose <u>you</u> all those years ago, that's why I've trained you and, dare I say, raised you into the young man I see before me. I wanted you to have the chance at a life I did not. One unburdened by the guilt of the survivor."

I shake my head. "But why bring me into SPRUNG, if that was the case? Why do any of this?"

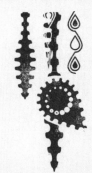

"I dare say, my dear boy," the Chairman sighs as he reaches into his pocket, "we all make mistakes. I thought at the time I could see myself in you. By disguising your sister's spirit, I could save you some of my pain. But I see now that was foolish. Even selfish."

MILLICENT
ALWAYS WITH
DOLL IN HAND ...

HER DOLL WAS USED
AT THE SÉANCE.

A shiver down my spine distracts me from the Chairman's mea culpas and draws my attention away. Behind the Chairman, I catch a glimpse of a caped figure, a silhouette I know well, slipping out of the Arrivals Hall. It's the silhouette of a man who is supposed to be in Tuscany gobbling truffles. Darko Mantich. The moment he's sure I'm watching him, Darko grins broadly. He raises a book in the air - the empty journal he stole from my bungalow down in Mexico - then nonchalantly tosses it into an airport rubbish bin. We lock eyes in another stare-down.

"Do you hear me, Ag? I have the label . . ." The Chairman pulls me back to him.

With a showman's flourish, he slips an item from his pocket like a magician pulling a rabbit from a hat. In the palm of his hand is a faded piece of paper.

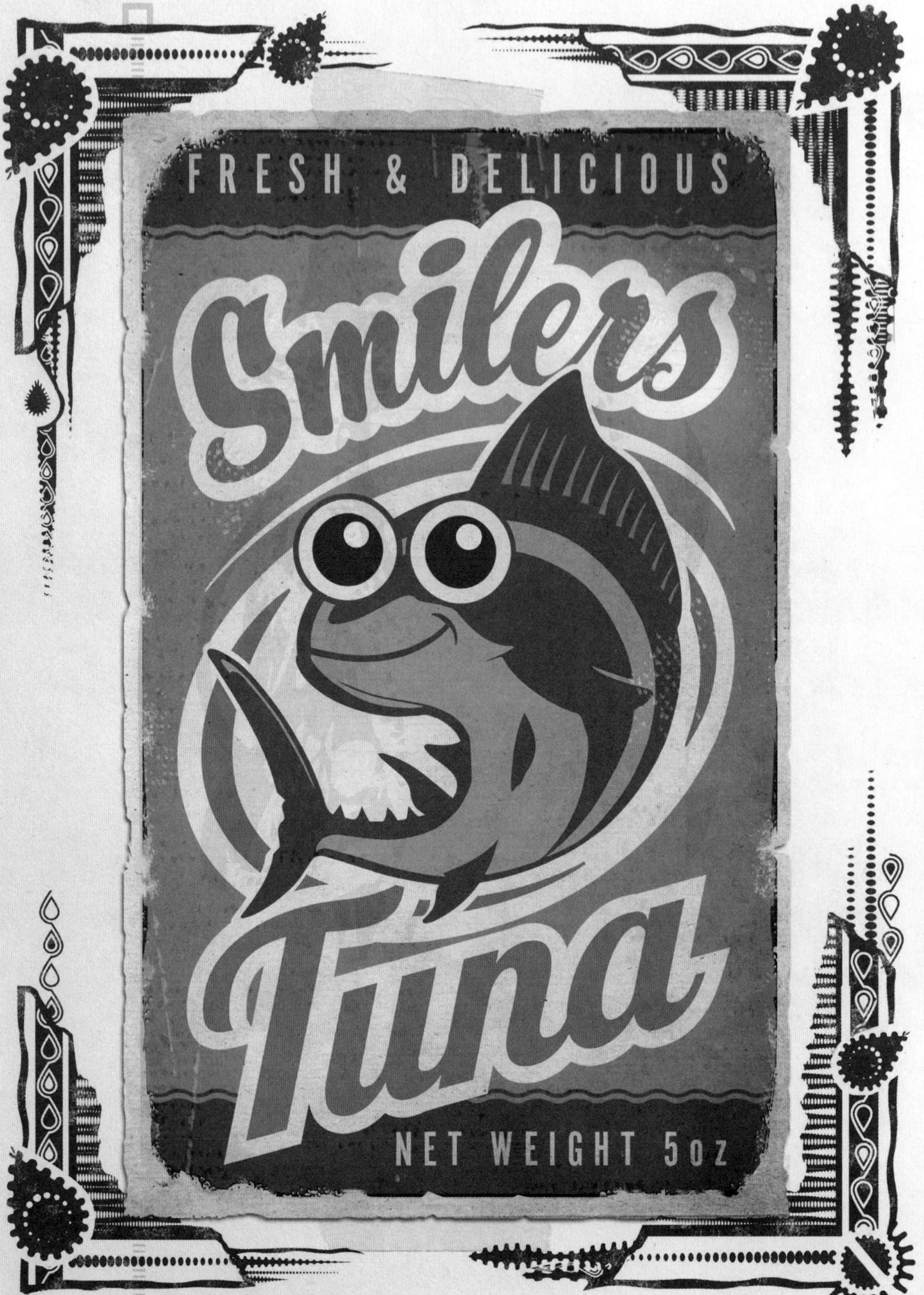
FRESH & DELICIOUS
Smilers
Tuna
NET WEIGHT 5oz

ELLIE'S SMILE

"It's time for Electra to rest, don't you think?"

I stare at the faded purple ink - illegible now. And on the front - the Smiler's tuna logo, still clear on the label. I meet the eyes of the old man before me, pleading - if that's possible.

"I only ever wanted you to be happy. Can you blame an old man for his foolish choice? To save a young boy?"

END OF CASE LOG

How could I believe him? Did it even matter? I took the label from his hands, gingerly, like plucking a flower too delicate to survive. Across the hall, Darko was gone. The Chairman remained right in front of me, but he might as well have gone too.

I stared down at the little smiling face on the label - the smile of the swimming fish - and saw clearly now that the smile was Ellie's all along.

PHANTASMIST

GHOSTKEEPER'S FINAL CASE OBSERVATIONS:

- I had a family after all. My sister saved me, and her spirit has been watching out for me. Now I must save her.
- After the Chairman left the airport, I went over to the rubbish bin where Darko had dropped the empty journal and picked up the book. Inside was a note.
- The note wasn't from Darko Mantich. It was signed HH.

ECTO-ENERGY TYPE
TOXIGON

CASE FILE

Gone for Good

CASE FILE:	25007
GHOSTKEEPER:	Agamemnon White
LOCATION:	Dearborn, Michigan, U.S.A.
PRELIMINARY OUTLINE:	August 11

I am not your enemy.

Trust me.

I beg you not to complete the
Spectral Flush.

The Ghoul is close.

H H

- I'm seeing ghouls everywhere now.
- Helani Hekili wants my trust.
- Nettie Dahl wants my forgiveness.
- The Chairman wants my . . . success? But why?
- Am I really willing to believe that Jeremiah Goodrough,
  Chairman of SPRUNG, only ever helped me to hurt me.
  Is that why he hid my sister from me?

Additional notes:

INTRODUCTION TO CASE ELEMENTS AND ODDITIES

- For years, there have been reports of atomic ecto-energy manifestations at the Dearborn State University reactor.
- This Toxigon manifestation is considered a HIGH DANGER target. It should only be undertaken with full knowledge of the risks.

WARNING: DEATH OR UNDEATH MAY RESULT!

I need to talk to someone I <u>can</u> trust.
I need to talk to Lily Zhang.

INITIAL OUTLINE OF ODD, WEIRD, AND OTHERWISE GHOSTLY BEHAVIOR

As I've previously written, finding Lily Zhang is impossible unless she wants to be found. Unless, that is, she finds you. I had gone into a coffee shop to call Lily and was making notes in my journal when she quite literally emerged from the armchair right beside me. Let me rephrase that - as Lily Zhang stood up, she simply stepped out of the armchair disguise she was wearing. I did mention she's a master of disguise as well as being SPRUNG's Chief Meta Technologist, didn't I?

"I need to speak with you, Agamemnon White."

LILY ZHANG,
MASTER OF DISGUISE

 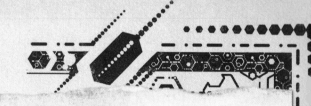

Additional notes:

11 August
9:32 a.m.

In person, Lily is like a tiny shrivelled bird with
immense attitude.

"Let me see your SPRUNG Ghost-o-Matic." She snatches
the device from me. Her tiny fingers fly across the
screen as she makes tut-tuts with her tongue.

And how did she know my password? "I've been tracking
some very unusual energy readings from your device - this
could do some serious damage . . ."

"But I haven't broken anything!"

"Yet!" She fixes me with her beady eye. "You
haven't broken anything <u>yet</u>. But if you carry on
like this . . ." She jabs at me with her bony
finger.

"You'll break *you*."

Lily Zhang already knows what the energy types
collected in my journal and recorded in my SPRUNG
Ghost-o-Matic can be used for. As I share with
her what I've learned about the Spectral Flush,
ghouls and the origins of SPRUNG, I get the
distinct feeling that I'm not telling her much
that she doesn't already know. After all, she was
there at the beginning. She knows what can happen.

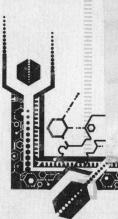
THE LAST TIME I BLINDLY FOLLOWED
LILY ZHANG PROVED PAINFUL

"My advice is simple. Burn the journal. Hide.
Come with me now." Lily starts toward the exit,
beckoning me to follow.

But she doesn't know about Ellie and how she saved my
life by losing hers. "I have to finish this. I have to
save my sister's spirit now."

"You are sure? Even if you might get broken?"

Additional notes:

HELANI HEKILI,
GHOULHUNTER.

"I'm not one of your inventions, Lily. You don't need to protect me."

Lily shakes her tiny old head. "You don't understand. To survive this, you might get broken anyway." She clasps my arm and pulls me away from the exit, toward the back of the coffee shop. "Believe me, Agamemnon White. If a ghoul is really on your trail, you don't just risk losing your life or your sister's spirit—you risk losing your living soul."

I follow her toward a rear door I didn't know was there.

"Well . . . that sounds pretty bad."

"It is. About as bad as anything could be."

Lily opens the rear door, letting in bright sunlight.

"Come on outside. There's someone I want you to meet."

A massive 2-metre frame steps into view, silhouetted by the sunlight. Lily Zhang looks like an ancient child next to the giant beside her, a weathered redwood tree of a woman, her features carved like a totem pole of flesh.

"Ag, let me introduce Helani Hekili."

"I've been watching you, Agamemnon White. You are a very talented Ghostkeeper."

"Yes, I am," I answer honestly.

Helani lets out a booming baritone of a laugh, though I wasn't being funny.

"Well, let's see if we can't teach you how to be a Ghoulhunter too."

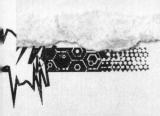

...IT'S NOW A LIBRARY WITH RARE BOOKS AND ONE VERY RARE TOXIGON.

ONCE A REACTOR WITH TOXIC WARNINGS...

INITIAL OUTLINE OF ODD, WEIRD, AND OTHERWISE GHOSTLY BEHAVIOR

 GHOSTKEEPER'S LOG - GHOSTKEEPER'S LOG - GHOSTKEEPER'S LOG

12 August
Dearborn, Michigan
9:28 a.m.

Dearborn State is one of the best universities in the world. It is also one of the largest. Almost 19,000 undergraduates and 13,000 postgraduate students attend in any given year. There are over 5,000 faculty in 484 major buildings, spread over 15,965 acres. And somewhere among all of those people and places, is the spirit of one extremely rare and dangerous ghost—the Toxigon.

I have come to DSU because its Toxigon is famous among Ghostkeepers. Students have been sharing images of the bizarre decorations on the Memorial Library via social media for several years - silhouettes like the ones that formed in Hiroshima after the A-bomb was dropped, marking the spot where people stood or played or strolled at that instant.

Additional notes:

I learned online that the memorial library on campus was previously the home of the Delano Nuclear Reactor. The project that built the reactor came with good intentions - in memory of those casualties from the Second World War, an institute was formed to study the peaceful use of nuclear energy, with the reactor at its core. Research was conducted for 60 years until the reactor was decommissioned in 2008.

It appears that Professor Alvin Backenhorn, who had run the nuclear facility for many years as Head of Nuclear Physics at the university, never appeared at the decommissioning ceremony. Later that day, it was discovered that the core had suffered a minor meltdown. Professor Backenhorn appeared to have heroically prevented the spread of radiation across the campus. No-one knew what had caused such a potential disaster.

The Head of Nuclear Physics vanished, and a shadow of a man, with a faint outline of his classic spectacles and mustache, appeared splayed across the side of the library's outside wall later that day. From time to time, the silhouette would be found in a new position on the wall.

Other than these silhouettes, this campus was like any other. There was no sign of the paranormal. For a moment, I sat with the sun on my back and imagined myself a normal 18-year-old, ready for freshman year at college. Nothing could ruin that perfect moment. Except, of course, for the arrival of Jeremiah Goodrough and Darko Mantich.

ALVIN BACKENHORN, PRESUMABLY BEFORE HE WAS UNDEAD.

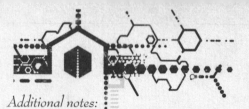
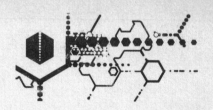

Additional notes:

Which is why I gave them both a false location where I was heading to find the Toxigon, a very long way from my true destination. So I could take my time, knowing how hard the task ahead of me would be.

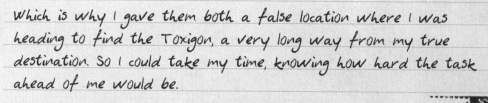

PRELIMINARY FINDINGS, SPOOKY OR OTHERWISE

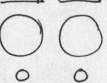

Dearborn State Student Union
12:43 p.m.

I am chewing very slowly to savour the tuna melt. It might be the best tuna melt I have ever eaten, even better than the ones Jean used to make. This may be, however, because I have realized it may be the last one I will ever enjoy.

My plan is simple, possibly brilliant, but also probably idiotic. There's a high chance I'll die. At best, I'll suffer. But I'll save my sister's spirit, give resolution to the ghosts I've collected, and maybe . . . just maybe . . . I might stop the Ghoul. If - it's a big if - I have the courage to go through with my simple, possibly brilliant, probably idiotic plan.

Campus Facilities Management Office
1:54 p.m.

My plan goes poorly from the very start. Constance Chung is the Facilities Manager for the university. Normally, when I flash my SPRUNG credentials, nobody really looks and assumes it's a law enforcement badge of some kind. I get the help I need from officials. But Miss Chung is quite meticulous. She reads the card carefully, speaking the words out loud:

"The Society for the Pursuit of the Reputedly Undead, Namely Ghosts. Hah! That's a new one!"

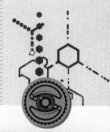

"I only need a few minutes in the files. It really is a matter of life and death . . . and undeath too, come to that."

Miss Chung gives me a glare, which then slowly dissolves into a wide grin.

"Wait a minute. You . . . you're from that show aren't you? *Pranks and Misdemeanors?* This is a joke, right?"

"I'm not very good at jokes, Miss Chung."

"Oh, I think you're very good. But you didn't fool me. I could smell something fishy . . ."

Perhaps Lily has been correct about my breath. But I go along with Miss Chung's assumption.

"Ha ha. Yes. You've got me. Big joke."

She notices my SPRUNG Ghost-o-Matic device. "Is that the camera?"

"Well, in a way. It's more of a paranormal scanner."

She's increasingly excited and is paying little attention to what I'm saying. This has happened to me before, of course.

MISS CHUNG SAW RIGHT THROUGH ME ... AND EVERYTHING ELSE.

"Is this because of all those claims the Memorial Library's haunted? Is that why you guys are doing this?"

"I'm sorry. Which guys?"

"Oh, right." Miss Chung gives me a big wink. It confuses me. "Wouldn't want to ruin your show. Okay, let's do this."

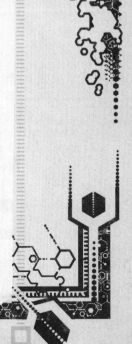

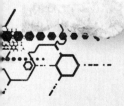

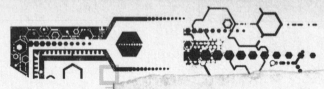

I am still unsure what Miss Chung wants me to do.

"Go on. Ask me again, About the undead . . ."

And that's when Miss Constance Chung tells me about the haunting of the old Delano Reactor building, now the Campus Memorial Library, by Professor Alvin Backenhorn. A one-time member of the research faculty, now deceased, and according to a number of students residing in the bowels of what was once the nuclear reactor, still off limits to all. __ _

"It was Professor Backenhorn's mistake. He was responsible for the core in the decommissioning. His calculations were off or something. And the fuel rods didn't cool like they were supposed to. It was pretty scary around here for a while."

"If it's off limits, how do students know he's there?"

"He pops out sometimes for doughnuts." Miss Chung winks at me and I furrow my brow. She sighs, losing patience with my lack of joking around. "I'm just kidding. It's stupid. It's just an old building, with old chemicals and equipment knocking around."

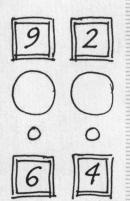

I know I am supposed to reassure her that I won't laugh at her, but that's not really me. I go with serious. It suits me.

NUCLEAR FUEL RODS— AS SCARY AS ANY GHOST.

"Seriously, how do they know, Miss Chung?"

For the first time, Miss Chung appears quite deadly serious too. "They say they know he's there because they can hear him scream."

S.P.R.U.N.G.

FROM THE DESK OF
JEREMIAH GOODROUGH

notes:

I've had some time to think through why Ag did what he did that day. And, of course, like you, I've read this journal. So I know he was coming to believe that a ghoul was on his tail. Even more than that, that he suspected that I might be that ghoul. Which explains why he told me to meet him not at the Memorial Library, but at the Port Authority bus terminal in Midtown Manhattan. Not a pleasant place to spend a few hours. I had a man wipe his hands on my lapels. However, I gather he sent Darko Mantich to a circus on the side of the road in New Jersey, so I suppose I should be grateful.

But he wasn't thinking clearly, and I sorely wish I had been there to stop him from taking the actions he chose over the next few hours; actions that would bring about his disappearance and lead us to these circumstances.

<u>Campus Memorial Library</u>

Connie Chung led me to the basement office of the late Professor Backenhorn, but wouldn't go any farther, as she said she found it "seriously creepy, even if you're cute." I was unclear what one had to do with the other, but I had no time to consider this.

The university had managed to keep the accident with the fuel rods under wraps. Indeed, I found that even using a Geiger counter revealed no sign of any radiation in the reactor building. Was Miss Chung just playing for the cameras she imagined I had brought with me? She had only let me leave her after I promised her I would let her know the TV show air date in advance and take her as a date to the premiere.

But the office still had files under the name Alvin Backenhorn. The papers were a mess - takeout menus, betting slips and calculations all mixed up together.

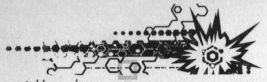

Was "Flavour Factor" the name of a horse, a theory, or a noodle dish?

There were photographs too, many of them showing equipment from the reactor. One photograph showed a series of dials on a bank of controls — someone had haphazardly drawn positions for the dials to be turned to on the image in pen, indicating the numbers for the correct setting. It was clearly drawn in haste, in the panic of discovery and mistake. A feeling I recognize well. When you find something too late. I made a note of the corrected numbers.

THE GHOST-O-MATIC DOESN'T HAVE A BUILT-IN GEIGER COUNTER.

I set off into the sub-basement of the building, my SPRUNG Ghost-o-Matic in one hand and my Geiger counter in the other. Multiple staircases, a number of 'no entry' signs, one heavily barricaded door, which mysteriously opens with a slight push. I keep moving. It's increasingly dark, and I'm soon able to see only by the glow of the screens on my devices. But there's still no reading to indicate any sign of radioactivity or paranormal energy. No sign of a chest. Nothing that looks like the photographs I've seen. Just empty cellars. I'm about to turn back and climb to the surface . . .

. . . when I hear the scream.

It's coming from under my feet. I can feel the floor vibrating. I look down and see a faint glow from lights in the floor. I get down on my hands and knees. The glowing comes from discs, dusty and hard to make out. I wipe the dust away with my handkerchief - the red one with the white polka dots - and reveal luminescent paint, like on old-fashioned glow-in-the-dark watch faces. These are dials in the floor. I can hear my own breath, the sound of my heart, as I reach down to touch them.

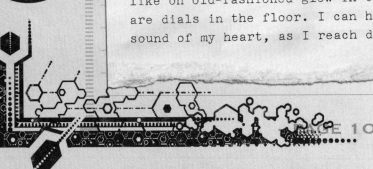

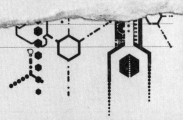

Then the alarms begin to sound. Both my Geiger counter and my SPRUNG Ghost-o-Matic whirr to life and begin to scream shrilly at me, lights blinking on and off, as if a dam is about to break.

Heat is rising from the floor tiles, and I'm sweating as I concentrate on the next steps. I begin to adjust the glowing dials. I remember to use the corrected numbers, not the numbers shown in the photograph . . . knowing that this will let me seek out the final ghost, the Toxigon who I can feel right beneath this panel in the cellar floor. But where is he?

I can hear the screams. More and more. That's when I realize I can hear another sound too. Something different. Laughter. Endless laughter mixing with the screams to rattle through the cellars. Is the laughter just inside my head?

Someone is happy I've found this ghost. Someone thinks that their grand plan is falling into place. Someone thinks that once again Agamemnon White is the butt of the joke. The butt of a joke the Ghoul created.

The thing is, I don't tend to get jokes. But I get this one. I don't think I have it in me to follow through, after all. I'd made up my mind to capture the Dearborn State Toxigon, knowing my body will be irradiated. The Ghoul would no longer want my ruined body as a host, but I just might live long enough to complete the journal and resolve the spirits, including my sister, Ellie. But I can't move. In this hot, dark place, I'm completely frozen. My glasses steam up. I can barely see . . .

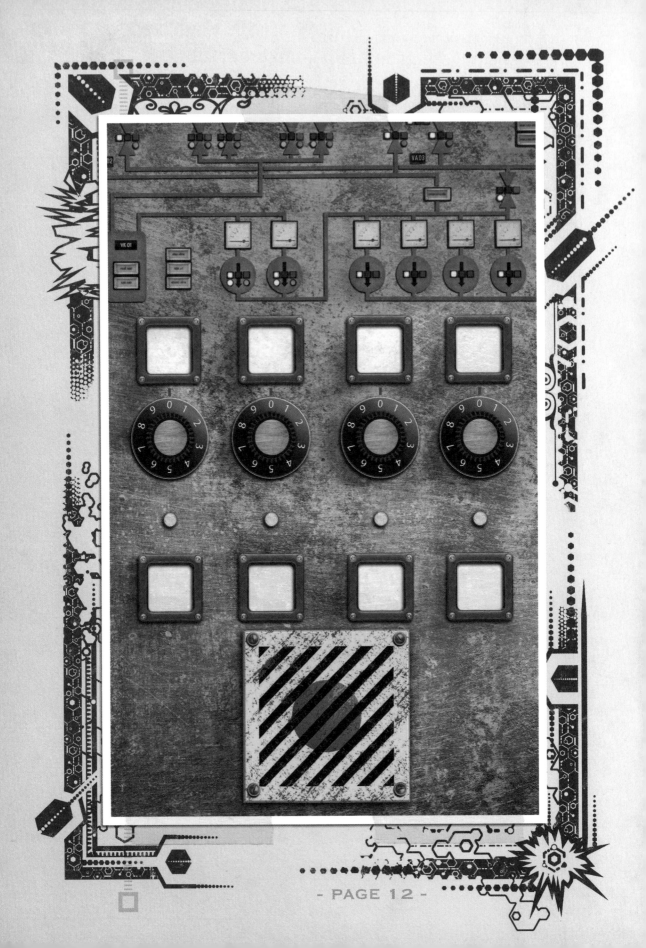

. . . but there's the faintest shape emerging on my left spectacle lens - a smiley face. Ellie's smiley face from endless windows and drinks and raindrops.

I reach down and force my fist through the shaking panels of the hatch on the floor, smashing it open. I expect a vast burst of light and flame from the buried fuel rods below, but instead I just see the dial of my Geiger counter go to the far end of RED as it emits a piercing alarm, then bursts into smoke. The readings have gone past deadly measures of nuclear exposure. I feel my skin begin to buzz, my insides are hot. And I'm face-to-face with the ghost of Alvin Backenhorn, the Toxigon.

But I am not scared. I've done what I must do.

END OF LOG

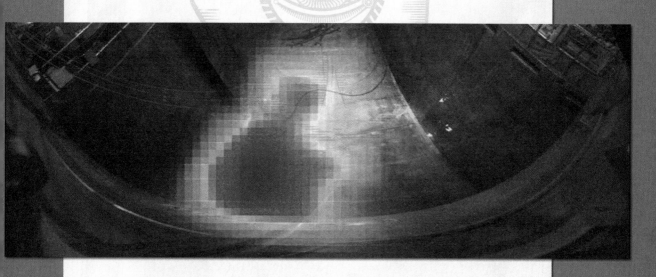

Over the days that followed, the silhouettes vanished from outside the library and no one heard the screams from the basement again. Miss Chung claimed the phenomena had all been a part of that prank show that set off the building alarms.

Some joke.

TOXIGON

GHOSTKEEPER'S FINAL CASE OBSERVATIONS:

- It's all in the letter.

I must say I've really enjoyed all this – it was fun the first time, keeping an eye on Agamemnon as he gradually built the perfect journal for my purposes, the precise power pack required for me to shift myself from this still magnificently bearded but otherwise shriveled husk of a body to take control of a young, healthy, and suitably positioned human vessel for my next hundred years. Ag's intuitive intelligence could feel something was off, but his detail-focused mind was distracted, as I knew it would be, by his heart.

Jeremiah was the same way at first, letting Madame D'Olivera Balding teach him and his friends the way to capture ghosts so he could reach out to the sister he lost. And once he knew the truth, when his fellow founders at SPRUNG were on my trail, I could still use his sister's spirit to keep him silent just long enough . . . and then it was too late. For him. He couldn't say a thing, because I, the great Ghoul, had moved from Mme D'Olivera to Jeremiah Goodrough and was in control of his every word, his every wink, his every waking moment.

The moment I met young Ag as a boy I knew I'd found a perfect replacement for Jeremiah when the time came. I could shape him and prepare him, like raising a beautiful flower . . . or a fatted calf. Such a shame he had to ruin it all in the end – and for what? He didn't even keep enough strength to complete the Resolution ceremony and save his sister's spirit. Boohoo, eh? Boohoo.

Anyway, that's not strictly true – sorry about that. I do have a tendency to lie a bit. Ag did survive long enough, might even have pulled through. Until I got ahold of him and made certain he was finished.

Upward and onward, as my previous vessel, Mme D'Olivera, used to say!

It's been great reliving my favorite moments of Ag's journey with you—that crazy cleaning lady vacuuming the walls, the waterfall up at Foggy Bottom that only targeted Ag, the flying pop-up toast. It got a bit grim toward the end there, with the nuclear power and radiation. But, as they say, you can't make an omelette without breaking a few eggs.

And you've been marvelous fun to watch too. Honestly, I'm amazed you're still here! How many warnings did you need that there was a ghoul behind this before you slammed the journal shut and ran? You're either staggeringly brave or incredibly stupid.

Well, I'm going to give you one last chance to show which one you are. I think I would have enjoyed being Agamemnon White – but you've shown yourself to be a more than adequate replacement.

So you can try to complete the Resolution ceremony and free the spirits you've collected to their well-earned rest . . . or you can leave the story for someone else to complete.

Because one way or another Jeremiah Goodrough's time is over. And not every Ghostkeeper will make the sacrifice Ag made – he chose to poison his own body and make it uninhabitable for a discerning ghoul like me. What about you? Will you make a sacrifice like that? I don't think so.

Of course all you have to do is complete the Resolution ceremony and release the energy of the ghosts before I can take that energy from you. Then you are the hero. Ag's sister El will be at peace at last. Ag himself will have sacrificed his life for good reasons. And you? Well, you never know, my colleagues might even ask you to stick around at SPRUNG.

And if you lose? Would it really be so bad? Sure, I'd be in charge and you'd have to mind your manners like dear old Jeremiah has for all these years – he's so quiet now I sometimes forget he's even here at all. But the things we'll do, the places we'll see, the ghosts we'll consume! Trust me, it's FUN being a ghoul. So what will it be, young Ghostkeeper?

Will you stick or twist? Stay or run? Win or lose?

Go on, give it a go . . . that's the spirit!

RESOLUTION

Once the Ghostkeeper's Journal contains the ecto-energy of five ghosts, it must be returned by the field operative to SPRUNG Archives for completion of the Resolution ceremony. This allows the ghosts within the Journal to finally reach the Beyond.

The Ghostkeeper enters the unique personal identification code from his or her Ghostkeeper Identity Card to provide the Archivist access to the ecto-energy inside the Journal.

☐ ☐ ☐ ☐

The Archivist must now enter a private code to initiate use of tools in the Ghostkeeper's Journal and the Ghost-o-Matic app which are required for the Resolution ceremony.

☐ ☐ ☐ ☐

ONCE COMPLETE, TURN THE PAGE TO COMMENCE RESOLUTION.

SPRUNG RESOLUTION CEREMONY

- Unlock the mechanism on the opposite page to draw the ecto-energy of all five spirits to the Resolution ceremony.

- Release the ecto-energies from their individual containers so they mix in the environment surrounding the Journal.

- Use the Ghost-o-Matic Lens to target and capture the newly combined and extremely powerful ecto-energy mixture.

- A full vial of the combined energy will provide sufficient power to force open a Portal from within the Journal to the Beyond.

- Turn to the Portal page, where ecto-printing facilitates the opening of the Portal. As the ghosts' energy is manipulated, its power weakens, so the Portal cannot remain stable for long. Work quickly to form the combined energy into its required shape—the symbol of the Society. The Eye.

- The Ghost-o-Matic forms a mechanical container, securing the shape of the Eye for its descent through the Portal to the Beyond, and final rest at last for the five ghosts it contains.

- The Resolution ceremony is complete.

- File the used Ghostkeeper's Journal in the SPRUNG Archives for historical reference and apparition tabulation.

COMPILED BY NETTIE DAHL, CHIEF ARCHIVIST

AB HOMINE, SPIRITUS
OUT OF THE MAN, THE GHOST

EX QUINQUE SPIRITUUM, OCULUS
FROM FIVE GHOSTS, AN EYE

PER OCULUM, FINEM
THROUGH THE EYE, THE END

On behalf of my fellow members of the Society for the Pursuit of the Reputedly Undead, Namely Ghosts, I offer you this official invitation to join our order and keep our secrets.

You have already shown yourself worthy of Ghostkeeper rank. We need operatives ready for the new challenges that the emergence of the Ghoul will bring.

From this day until the Ghoul is gone, I will be on the monster's evil trail. I hope you will join me on this journey. For now, however, you must rest and prepare yourself. I enclose your SPRUNG membership credentials, based on your achievements in following Agamemnon White's path.

You have earned our gratitude and our trust. But always remember the words of our new Chairman, Helani Hekili: "Never trust what you can't see with your own eyes."

THE GHOSTKEEPER'S JOURNAL
AND FIELD GUIDE

THIS IS A CARLTON BOOK

Concept, text and characters
© Polarity Reversal Limited 2018

Book design, illustration, and Augmented Reality app
© Carlton Books Limited 2018

Published in 2018 by Carlton Books Limited,
an imprint of the Carlton Publishing Group,
20 Mortimer Street, London W1T 3JW

A catalogue record for this book is available
from the British Library.

ISBN: 978-1-78312-398-8

Printed in China
1 2 3 4 5 6 7 8 9 10

A ROSTER OF SPRUNG OPERATIVES WHO HAVE
CONTRIBUTED TO THIS JOURNAL

CREATOR, AUTHOR AND CHIEF TOAST-EATER:
Japhet Asher

ADDITIONAL CASE FILE WRITER & LEAD TUNA ENTHUSIAST:
Chelsea Asher

DESIGN DIRECTOR AND HERDER OF THE PARANORMAL:
Russell Porter

DESIGN AND ECTO-PRINTING:
Jon Lucas & Carol Wright

DIGITAL PRODUCER AND APPARITION MANAGER:
Will Jones

APP DEVELOPMENT AND META-TECHNOLOGY:
Phil Hoskins & Scary Beasties Ltd

EXECUTIVE EDITORS AND APPARITION EXECUTORS:
Alexandra Koken & Joff Brown

CONSULTING EDITOR AND ASTRO-MANIPULATOR:
Gabrielle Balkan

PRODUCTION AND CONDENSATION EXPERT:
Nicola Davey

The Society wishes to express its eternal gratitude to *Cathy "Spooky Moon" Raymond*,
Jonathan "Powers" Goodman, *Russell "Lavage" McLean*, *Dashiell "Father of the Toxigon" Asher*, and
the Friendly Colonel of Rainham Hall, for their inspiration and ecto-Sense.

The publishers would like to thank the following sources for their kind permission to reproduce the pictures in this book.

Front cover Shutterstock, back cover NDSU Archives, pg2. Public Domain, pg4. NDSU Archives, pg5. liveauctioneers.com, pg6. 3355m/Shutterstock, pg8. Public Domain, pg9. Hoch2wo/Alamy Stock Vector, pg11 © 2018 by Auction Team Breker, Cologne, Germany, www.breker.com, pg19. NDSU Archives, pg20 (top) Library of Congress, (bottom) pg21 (top), 21 (bottom), Public Domain, pg24. Hoch2wo/Alamy Stock Vector; Case File [The Dentist] pg1 (left) Vladimir Gjorgiev/Shutterstock, (centre) Wayhome Studio/Shutterstock, (right) Palmer Jane LLC/Shutterstock, pg2 Mochipet/Shutterstock, pg3 (top) Tefi/Shutterstock , (right) Stocktrek Images, Inc./Alamy Stock Photo, (bottom) Thomas Trutschel/Photothek via Getty Images, pg4 Kotin/Shutterstock, pg7 (top) ClassicStock/Alamy Stock Photo, pg8 Chepko Danil Vitalevich/Shutterstock, pg11 Melica/Shutterstock, pg12 Valentin Agapov/Shutterstock, pg13 Public Domain, pg14 (left, centre) Puwadol Jaturawutthichai/Shutterstock, (right) Kassaraporn/Shutterstock; Case File [The Muse] intro Andreas Solaro/AFP/Getty Images, pg1 S-F/Shutterstock, pg3 Public Domain, pg5 Marze/Shutterstock, pg6 Frank Kletschkus/Alamy Stock Photo, pg7 & pg8 Shutterstock, pg10 Public Domain, pg11 (top) Getty Images, pg12 Anne Murphy/Alamy Stock Photo; Case File [Runaway] intro (top left) Simonprw/Stockimo/Alamy Stock Photo, (top right) Steven May/Stockimo/Alamy Stock Photo, (centre left) Photo by Manos Gkika on Unsplash, (centre) Photo by Scott Rodgerson on Unsplash, (right) Sundays Photography/Shutterstock, (bottom) Jozef Klopacka/Shutterstock, pg1 (top) cookingpanda.com, (bottom) DG Stock/Shutterstock, pg2 Steve Heap/Shutterstock, pg3 Lisa F. Young/Shutterstock, pg4 Everett Collection/ Shutterstock, pg5 Premkamon/Shutterstock, pg6 Maria Dryfhout, pg8 Getty Images, pg9 Brent Hofacker/Shutterstock, pg10 Van Hilbersum/Alamy Stock Photo, Case File [Toast Ghost] pg1 & 2 (bottom) Chones/Shutterstock, pg3 everyfoodweeat, pg4 (left) Red Spruce/Shutterstock, (bottom) Private Collection, pg5 (top right) Mary Evans Picture Library, (centre) ChervovRV/ Shutterstock, pg6 ClassicStock/Alamy Stock Photo, pg7 SMAK_Photo/ Shutterstock, pg10 Jira Po/Shutterstock, pg11 Getty Images, pg13 (top) Everett Collection/Shutterstock, (bottom) Artur Balytskyi/Shutterstock; Surprise! JFunk/Shutterstock; Case File [Runaway part 2], pg2 Ken Biggs/ Alamy Stock Photo, pg3 Private Collection, pg4 (top) Wavebreakmedia Ltd PH104/Alamy Stock Photo, (bottom) Ryan Cardone/Stockimo/Alamy Stock Photo, pg5 Kirayonak Yuliya/Shutterstock, pg6 Remy Boprey/Alamy Stock Photo, pg7 (top) Getty Images, (bottom) Diego Grandi/Alamy Stock Photo, pg8 Maximilian Stimmel/Alamy Stock Photo, pg9 Mr Max/Shutterstock, pg10 Public Domain, pg12 Everett Collection/Shutterstock, pg13 Photo by Aimee Vogelsang on Unsplash; Case File [Gone for Good], pg1 A Dreamer/ Shutterstock, pg2 Skusku/Alamy Stock Photo, pg3 Manuel "Manny" Librodo Jr., p3 (top) GFC Collection/Alamy Stock Photo, (bottom) RikoBest/ Shutterstock, pg4 Gado Images/Alamy Stock Photo, pg7 & pg8 Getty Images, pg10 Newscom/Alamy Stock Photo, pg11 Ian Rutherford/Alamy Stock Photo, pg13 Public Domain; Chief Ghoulhunter photo Neil Lang/Shutterstock

Illustrators: Leo Brown, Carol Wright, Jon Lucas and Russell Porter

Every effort has been made to acknowledge correctly and contact the source and/or copyright holder of each picture and Carlton Books Limited apologises for any unintentional errors or omissions, which will be corrected in future editions of this book.

CARLTON
BOOKS